CONTENTS

501346058

EDITORIAL DIRECTOR Justin Kestler
EXECUTIVE EDITOR Ben Florman

SERIES EDITORS Boomie Aglietti, John Crowther, Justin Kestler
PRODUCTION Christian Lorentzen

WRITER John Henriksen
EDITORS Matt Blanchard, John Crowther

This edition published by Spark Publishing

Spark Publishing
A Division of SparkNotes LLC
120 Fifth Avenue, 8th Floor
New York, NY 10011

04 05 SN 9 8 7 6 5 4 3 2

Please send all comments and questions or report errors to
feedback@sparknotes.com.

Library of Congress information available upon request

Printed and bound in the United States

RRD-C

ISBN 1-58663-823-8

CONTEXT

L EV (LEO) NIKOLAEVICH TOLSTOY WAS BORN into a large and wealthy Russian landowning family in 1828, on the family estate of Yasnaya Polyana. Tolstoy's mother died when he was only two years old, and he idealized her memory throughout his life. Some critics speculate that the early loss of his mother colors Tolstoy's portrayal of the young Seryozha in *Anna Karenina*. When Tolstoy was nine, the family moved to Moscow. Shortly afterward his father died, murdered while traveling. Being orphaned before the age of ten, albeit without financial worries, left Tolstoy with an acute awareness of the power of death—an idea central to all his great works and especially evident in the strong association of the character of Anna Karenina with mortality.

Though an intelligent child, Tolstoy had little interest in academics. His aunt had to work hard to persuade him to go to university, and he failed his entrance exam on his first attempt. Eventually matriculating at Kazan University at the age of sixteen, Tolstoy studied law and Oriental languages. He showed interest in the grand heroic cultures of Persia, Turkey, and the Caucasus—an interest that persisted throughout his life. He was not popular at the university, and was self-conscious about his large nose and thick eyebrows. Ultimately, Tolstoy was dissatisfied with his education, and he left in 1847 without a degree. The social awkwardness of Konstantin Levin at the beginning of *Anna Karenina* reflects Tolstoy's own discomfort in fancy social surroudings at this time in his life.

In 1851, Tolstoy visited his brother in the Russian army and then decided to enlist shortly afterward. He served in the Crimean War (1854–1856) and recorded his experience in his *Sevastopol Stories* (1855). Tolstoy was able to write during his time in the army, producing a well-received autobiographical novel, *Childhood* (1852), followed by two others, *Boyhood* (1854) and *Youth* (1857). He ultimately evolved antimilitaristic feelings that can be seen in his implicit criticism of enthusiasm for the Slavic war in the final section of *Anna Karenina*.

In 1862, Tolstoy married Sofya Andreevna Behrs. He devoted most of the next two decades to raising a large family, managing his estate, and writing his two greatest novels, *War and Peace* (1865–

1869) and *Anna Karenina* (1875–1877). Levin's courtship of Kitty Shcherbatskaya in *Anna Karenina* was modeled on Tolstoy's own courtship of Sofya Andreevna, down to details such as the forgotten shirt that delays Levin's wedding.

In the years just prior to his marriage, Tolstoy had visited western Europe, partly to observe educational methods abroad. Upon returning, he founded and taught at schools for his peasants. His contact with his peasants led to a heightened appreciation for their morality, camaraderie, and enjoyment of life. Indeed, Tolstoy became quite critical of the superficiality of upper-class Russians, as we can see in Levin's discomfort with urban high society in *Anna Karenina*. Ultimately, Tolstoy developed a desire to seek spiritual regeneration by renouncing his family's possessions, much to the dismay of his long-suffering wife.

Tolstoy's life spanned a period of intense development for his home country. By the time of Tolstoy's death in 1910, Russia had transformed from a backward agricultural economy into a major industrialized world power. This period witnessed major debates between two intellectual groups in Russia: the Slavophiles, who believed Russian culture and institutions to be exceptional and superior to European culture, and the Westernizers, who believed that Russia needed to follow more liberal, Western modes of thought and government. We see traces of this debate about the destiny of Russia—whether it should join Europe in its march toward secular values and scientific thought or reject modernization and cherish the traditional, Asiatic elements of its culture—in *Anna Karenina*. Levin's peasants' preference for simple wooden plows over more efficient, modern agricultural tools symbolizes Russia's rejection of the West. We also see this cultural clash in the novel's portrait of the highly rational and ultra-Western bureaucrat Karenin—cool and efficient but also passionless.

During this time, Russia was also undergoing a crisis of political thought, with a series of authoritarian tsars provoking liberal and radical intellectuals who demanded European constitutional rights—or even revolution—in Russia. Tolstoy's ambivalent portrayal of the local elections in *Anna Karenina* demonstrates his uncertainty about the potential for democracy in Russia: the vote evokes much enthusiasm among the noblemen, but it also appears ineffectual and even pointless.

Tolstoy's eventual turn to religion in his own life left an imprint on all his later writings. Works such as *A Confession* (1882) and

The Kingdom of God Is Within You (1893) focused on the biblical Gospels' ideals of brotherly love and nonresistance to evil. *Anna Karenina* is often viewed as the turning point in Tolstoy's career, the point at which he shifted away from fiction and toward faith. The tug-of-war between these two forces helps create the rich portrait of Anna, whom Tolstoy both disapproves of and loves. Levin emerges as the voice of faith in the novel, with his final statement of the meaning of life corresponding closely to Tolstoy's own philosophy.

By the 1890s, Tolstoy's reputation as a prophet of social thought attracted disciples to his estate at Yasnaya Polyana seeking his wisdom. In 1898, Tolstoy published a radical essay called *What Is Art?*, in which he argued that the sole aim of great art must be moral instruction, and that on these grounds Shakespeare's plays and even Tolstoy's own novels are artistic failures. Frustrated by the disparity between his personal moral philosophy and his wealth, and by his frequent quarrels with his wife, Tolstoy secretly left home in November 1910, at the age of eighty-two. He fell ill with pneumonia along the way and died several days later in a faraway railway station. Tolstoy was mourned by admirers and followers around the world, and to this day is regarded as one of the greatest novelists in history.

A NOTE ON RUSSIAN NAMES

To English-speaking readers, the names of the characters in *Anna Karenina* may be somewhat confusing, as there are a number of name-related conventions in Russian that do not exist in English.

Each Russian has a first name, a patronymic, and a surname. A person's patronymic consists of his or her father's first name accompanied by a suffix meaning "son of" or "daughter of." Hence, Levin is addressed as Konstantin Dmitrich (son of Dmitri), Kitty is called Ekaterina Alexandrovna (daughter of Alexander), and so on. Characters in the novel frequently address each other in this formal manner, using both the first name and patronymic.

When characters do not address each other formally, they may use informal nicknames, or diminutives. Sometimes, these nicknames bear little resemblance to the characters' full names. For instance, Levin is sometimes called Kostya (the standard nickname for Konstantin), and Vronsky is sometimes called Alyosha (the diminutive of Alexei).

Furthermore, surnames in Russian take on both masculine and feminine forms. In *Anna Karenina,* for instance, Karenin's wife's surname takes the feminine form, Karenina. Likewise, Oblonsky's wife has the surname Oblonskaya, and their sons have the surname Oblonsky while their daughters have the surname Oblonskaya.

Keeping these conventions in mind helps to distinguish characters as they are addressed by different names throughout the novel. However, the use of these conventions varies in different editions of *Anna Karenina,* as some translators choose to simplify or eliminate name variants in order to make the novel more accessible to an English-speaking audience.

Plot Overview

THE OBLONSKY FAMILY OF MOSCOW is torn apart by adultery. Dolly Oblonskaya has caught her husband, Stiva, having an affair with their children's former governess, and threatens to leave him. Stiva is somewhat remorseful but mostly dazed and uncomprehending. Stiva's sister, Anna Karenina, wife of the St. Petersburg government official Karenin, arrives at the Oblonskys' to mediate. Eventually, Anna is able to bring Stiva and Dolly to a reconciliation.

Meanwhile, Dolly's younger sister, Kitty, is courted by two suitors: Konstantin Levin, an awkward landowner, and Alexei Vronsky, a dashing military man. Kitty turns down Levin in favor of Vronsky, but not long after, Vronsky meets Anna Karenina and falls in love with her instead of Kitty. The devastated Kitty falls ill. Levin, depressed after having been rejected by Kitty, withdraws to his estate in the country. Anna returns to St. Petersburg, reflecting on her infatuation with Vronsky, but when she arrives home she dismisses it as a fleeting crush.

Vronsky, however, follows Anna to St. Petersburg, and their mutual attraction intensifies as Anna begins to mix with the free-thinking social set of Vronsky's cousin Betsy Tverskaya. At a party, Anna implores Vronsky to ask Kitty's forgiveness; in response, he tells Anna that he loves her. Karenin goes home from the party alone, sensing that something is amiss. He speaks to Anna later that night about his suspicions regarding her and Vronsky, but she curtly dismisses his concerns.

Some time later, Vronsky participates in a military officers' horse race. Though an accomplished horseman, he makes an error during the race, inadvertently breaking his horse's back. Karenin notices his wife's intense interest in Vronsky during the race. He confronts Anna afterward, and she candidly admits to Karenin that she is having an affair and that she loves Vronsky. Karenin is stunned.

Kitty, meanwhile, attempts to recover her health at a spa in Germany, where she meets a pious Russian woman and her do-gooder protégée, Varenka. Kitty also meets Levin's sickly brother Nikolai, who is also recovering at the spa.

Levin's intellectual half-brother, Sergei Koznyshev, visits Levin in the country and criticizes him for quitting his post on the local administrative council. Levin explains that he resigned because he found the work bureaucratic and useless. Levin works enthusiastically with the peasants on his estate but is frustrated by their resistance to agricultural innovations. He visits Dolly, who tempts him with talk of reviving a relationship with Kitty. Later, Levin meets Kitty at a dinner party at the Oblonsky household, and the two feel their mutual love. They become engaged and marry.

Karenin rejects Anna's request for a divorce. He insists that they maintain outward appearances by staying together. Anna moves to the family's country home, however, away from her husband. She encounters Vronsky often, but their relationship becomes clouded after Anna reveals she is pregnant. Vronsky considers resigning his military post, but his old ambitions prevent him.

Karenin, catching Vronsky at the Karenin country home one day, finally agrees to divorce. Anna, in her childbirth agony, begs for Karenin's forgiveness, and he suddenly grants it. He leaves the divorce decision in her hands, but she resents his generosity and does not ask for a divorce. Instead, Anna and Vronsky go to Italy, where they lead an aimless existence. Eventually, the two return to Russia, where Anna is spurned by society, which considers her adultery disgraceful. Anna and Vronsky withdraw into seclusion, though Anna dares a birthday visit to her young son at Karenin's home. She begins to feel great jealousy for Vronsky, resenting the fact that he is free to participate in society while she is housebound and scorned.

Married life brings surprises for Levin, including his sudden lack of freedom. When Levin is called away to visit his dying brother Nikolai, Kitty sparks a quarrel by insisting on accompanying him. Levin finally allows her to join him. Ironically, Kitty is more helpful to the dying Nikolai than Levin is, greatly comforting him in his final days.

Kitty discovers she is pregnant. Dolly and her family join Levin and Kitty at Levin's country estate for the summer. At one point, Stiva visits, bringing along a friend, Veslovsky, who irks Levin by flirting with Kitty. Levin finally asks Veslovsky to leave. Dolly decides to visit Anna, and finds her radiant and seemingly very happy. Dolly is impressed by Anna's luxurious country home but disturbed by Anna's dependence on sedatives to sleep. Anna still awaits a divorce.

Levin and Kitty move to Moscow to await the birth of their baby, and they are astonished at the expenses of city life. Levin makes a

trip to the provinces to take part in important local elections, in which the vote brings a victory for the young liberals. One day, Stiva takes Levin to visit Anna, whom Levin has never met. Anna enchants Levin, but her success in pleasing Levin only fuels her resentment toward Vronsky. She grows paranoid that Vronsky no longer loves her. Meanwhile, Kitty enters labor and bears a son. Levin is confused by the conflicting emotions he feels toward the infant. Stiva goes to St. Petersburg to seek a cushy job and to beg Karenin to grant Anna the divorce he once promised her. Karenin, following the advice of a questionable French psychic, refuses.

Anna picks a quarrel with Vronsky, accusing him of putting his mother before her and unfairly postponing plans to go to the country. Vronsky tries to be accommodating, but Anna remains angry. When Vronsky leaves on an errand, Anna is tormented. She sends him a telegram urgently calling him home, followed by a profusely apologetic note. In desperation, Anna drives to Dolly's to say good-bye, and then returns home. She resolves to meet Vronsky at the train station after his errand, and she rides to the station in a stupor. At the station, despairing and dazed by the crowds, Anna throws herself under a train and dies.

Two months later, Sergei's book has finally been published, to virtually no acclaim. Sergei represses his disappointment by joining a patriotic upsurge of Russian support for Slavic peoples attempting to free themselves from Turkish rule. Sergei, Vronsky, and others board a train for Serbia to assist in the cause. Levin is skeptical of the Slavic cause, however.

Kitty becomes worried by Levin's gloomy mood. He has become immersed in questions about the meaning of life but feels unable to answer them. One day, however, a peasant remarks to Levin that the point of life is not to fill one's belly but to serve God and goodness. Levin receives this advice as gospel, and his life is suddenly transformed by faith.

Later that day, Levin, Dolly, and Dolly's children seek shelter from a sudden, violent thunderstorm, only to discover that Kitty and Levin's young son are still outside. Levin runs to the woods and sees a huge oak felled by lightning. He fears the worst, but his wife and child are safe. For the first time, Levin feels real love for his son, and Kitty is pleased. Levin reflects again that the meaning of his life lies in the good that he can put into it.

CHARACTER LIST

Anna Arkadyevna Karenina A beautiful, aristocratic married woman from St. Petersburg whose pursuit of love and emotional honesty makes her an outcast from society. Anna's adulterous affair catapults her into social exile, misery, and finally suicide. Anna is a beautiful person in every sense: intelligent and literate, she reads voraciously, writes children's books, and shows an innate ability to appreciate art. Physically ravishing yet tastefully reserved, she captures the attentions of virtually everyone in high society. Anna believes in love—not only romantic love but family love and friendship as well, as we see from her devotion to her son, her fervent efforts to reconcile Stiva and Dolly Oblonsky in their marital troubles, and her warm reception of Dolly at her country home. Anna abhors nothing more than fakery, and she comes to regard her husband, Karenin, as the very incarnation of the fake, emotionless conventionality she despises.

Alexei Alexandrovich Karenin Anna's husband, a high-ranking government minister and one of the most important men in St. Petersburg. Karenin is formal and duty-bound. He is cowed by social convention and constantly presents a flawless façade of a cultivated and capable man. There is something empty about almost everything Karenin does in the novel, however: he reads poetry but has no poetic sentiments, he reads world history but seems remarkably narrow-minded. He cannot be accused of being a poor husband or father, but he shows little tenderness toward his wife, Anna, or his son, Seryozha. He fulfills these family roles as he does other duties on his list of social obligations. Karenin's primary motivation in both his career and his personal life is self-preservation. When

8

he unexpectedly forgives Anna on what he believes may be her deathbed, we see a hint of a deeper Karenin ready to emerge. Ultimately, however, the bland bureaucrat remains the only Karenin we know.

Alexei Kirillovich Vronsky A wealthy and dashing military officer whose love for Anna prompts her to desert her husband and son. Vronsky is passionate and caring toward Anna but clearly disappointed when their affair forces him to give up his dreams of career advancement. Vronsky, whom Tolstoy originally modeled on the Romantic heroes of an earlier age of literature, has something of the idealistic loner in him. Yet there is a dark spot at the core of his personality, as if Tolstoy refuses to let us get too close to Vronsky's true nature. Indeed, Tolstoy gives us far less access to Vronsky's thoughts than to other major characters in the novel. We can never quite forget Vronsky's early jilting of Kitty Shcherbatskaya, and we wonder whether he feels guilt about nearly ruining her life. Even so, Vronsky is more saintly than demonic at the end of the novel, and his treatment of Anna is impeccable, even if his feelings toward her cool a bit.

Konstantin Dmitrich Levin A socially awkward but generous-hearted landowner who, along with Anna, is the co-protagonist of the novel. Whereas Anna's pursuit of love ends in tragedy, Levin's long courtship of Kitty Shcherbatskaya ultimately ends in a happy marriage. Levin is intellectual and philosophical but applies his thinking to practical matters such as agriculture. He aims to be sincere and productive in whatever he does, and resigns from his post in local government because he sees it as useless and bureaucratic. Levin is a figurehead in the novel for Tolstoy himself, who modeled Levin and Kitty's courtship on his own marriage. Levin's declaration of faith at the end of the novel sums up Tolstoy's own convictions, marking the start of the deeply religious phase of Tolstoy's life that followed his completion of *Anna Karenina*.

Ekaterina Alexandrovna Shcherbatskaya (Kitty) A beautiful young woman who is courted by both Levin and Vronsky, and who ultimately marries Levin. Modeled on Tolstoy's real-life wife, Kitty is sensitive and perhaps a bit overprotected, shocked by some of the crude realities of life, as we see in her horrified response to Levin's private diaries. But despite her indifference to intellectual matters, Kitty displays great courage and compassion in the face of death when caring for Levin's dying brother Nikolai.

Stepan Arkadyich Oblonsky (Stiva) Anna's brother, a pleasure-loving aristocrat and minor government official whose affair with his children's governess nearly destroys his marriage. Stiva and Anna share a common tendency to place personal fulfillment over social duties. Stiva is incorrigible, proceeding from his affair with the governess—which his wife, Dolly, honorably forgives—to a liaison with a ballerina. For Tolstoy, Stiva's moral laxity symbolizes the corruptions of big-city St. Petersburg life and contrasts with the powerful moral conscience of Levin. However, despite his transgressions, the affable Stiva is a difficult character to scorn.

Darya Alexandrovna Oblonskaya (Dolly) Stiva's wife and Kitty's older sister. Dolly is one of the few people who behave kindly toward Anna after her affair becomes public. Dolly's sympathetic response to Anna's situation and her guarded admiration for Anna's attempt to live her life fully hint at the positive aspects of Anna's experience. Well acquainted with the hardships of matrimony and motherhood, Dolly is, more than anyone else in the novel, in a position to appreciate what Anna has left behind by leaving with Vronsky. The novel opens with the painful revelation that Dolly's husband has betrayed her, and her even more painful awareness that he is not very repentant.

Sergei Alexeich Karenin (Seryozha) Karenin and Anna's young
son. Seryozha is a good-natured boy, but his father
treats him coldly after learning of Anna's affair. Anna
shows her devotion to Seryozha when she risks
everything to sneak back into the Karenin household
simply to bring birthday presents to her son.

Nikolai Dmitrich Levin Levin's sickly, thin brother. The
freethinking Nikolai is largely estranged from his
brothers, but over the course of the novel he starts to
spend more time with Levin. Nikolai is representative
of liberal social thought among certain Russian
intellectuals of the period; his reformed-prostitute
girlfriend, Marya Nikolaevna, is living proof of his
unconventional, radically democratic viewpoint.

Sergei Ivanovich Koznyshev Levin's half-brother, a famed
intellectual and writer whose thinking Levin has
difficulty following. Koznyshev embodies cold
intellectualism and is unable to embrace the fullness of
life, as we see when he cannot bring himself to propose
to Varenka.

Agafya Mikhailovna Levin's former nurse, now his trusted
housekeeper.

Countess Vronsky Vronsky's judgmental mother.

Alexander Kirillovich Vronsky Vronsky's brother.

Varvara Vronsky Alexander Vronsky's wife.

Prince Alexander Dmitrievich Shcherbatsky The practical
aristocrat father of Kitty, Dolly, and Natalie. Prince
Shcherbatsky favors Levin over Vronsky as a potential
husband for Kitty.

Princess Shcherbatskaya Kitty, Dolly, and Natalie's mother.
Princess Shcherbatskaya initially urges Kitty to favor
Vronsky over Levin as a suitor.

Countess Lydia Ivanovna A morally upright woman who is initially Anna's friend and later her fiercest critic. Hypocritically, the religious Lydia Ivanovna cannot bring herself to forgive or even to speak to the "fallen woman" Anna. Lydia Ivanovna harbors a secret love for Karenin, and induces him to believe in and rely on psychics.

Elizaveta Fyodorovna Tverskaya (Betsy) A wealthy friend of Anna's and Vronsky's cousin. Betsy has a reputation for wild living and moral looseness.

Marya Nikolaevna A former prostitute saved by Nikolai Levin, whose companion she becomes.

Madame Stahl A seemingly devout invalid woman whom the Shcherbatskys meet at a German spa. Madame Stahl appears righteous and pious, but Prince Shcherbatsky and others doubt her motivations.

Varvara Andreevna (Varenka) A pure and high-minded young woman who becomes Kitty's friend at the German spa. Varenka, who is a protégée of Madame Stahl, nearly receives a marriage proposal from Koznyshev.

Yashvin Vronsky's wild friend from the army. Yashvin has a propensity for losing large sums of money at gambling.

Nikolai Ivanovich Sviyazhsky A friend of Levin who lives in a far-off province.

Fyodor Vassilyevich Katavasov Levin's intellectual friend from his university days.

Vasenka Veslovsky A young, pleasant, somewhat dandyish man whom Stiva brings to visit Levin. The attentions Veslovsky lavishes on Kitty make Levin jealous.

Landau A French psychic who instructs Karenin to reject Anna's plea for a divorce.

Analysis of Major Characters

Anna Karenina

Originally conceived of as a dumpy and vulgar housewife, Anna evolved in successive versions of Tolstoy's manuscript into the beautiful, passionate, and educated woman we know in the novel. Tolstoy's increasing sympathy for this adulteress suggests the mixed feelings he harbored toward her: she is guilty of desecrating her marriage and home, but is noble and admirable nonetheless. The combination of these traits is a major reason for the appeal of this novel for more than a century. Anna is intelligent and literate, a reader of English novels and a writer of children's books. She is elegant, always understated in her dress. Her many years with Karenin show her capable of playing the role of cultivated, beautiful, society wife and hostess with great poise and grace. She is very nearly the ideal aristocratic Russian wife of the 1870s.

Yet we are ultimately impressed less by Anna's ideal attributes than by her passionate spirit and determination to live life on her own terms. Anna is a feminist heroine of sorts, riding on horseback in an era when such an activity was deemed suitable for men only. Disgraced, she dares to face St. Petersburg high society and refuses the exile to which she has been condemned, attending the opera when she knows very well she will meet with nothing but scorn and derision. Anna is a martyr to the old-fashioned Russian patriarchal system and its double standard for male and female adultery. Her brother, Stiva, is far looser in his morals but is never even chastised for his womanizing, whereas Anna is sentenced to social exile and suicide. Moreover, Anna is deeply devoted to her family and children, as we see when she sneaks back into her former home to visit her son on his birthday. Anna's refusal to lose Seryozha is the only reason she refuses Karenin's offer of divorce, even though this divorce would give her freedom.

The governing principle of Anna's life is that love is stronger than anything, even duty. She is powerfully committed to this principle. She rejects Karenin's request that she stay with him simply to maintain outward appearances of an intact marriage and family. Anna's greatest worry in the later stages of her relationship with Vronsky is that he no longer loves her but remains with her out of duty only. Her exile from civilized society in the later part of the novel is a symbolic rejection of all the social conventions we normally accept dutifully. She insists on following her heart alone. For Tolstoy, this mindset smacks of selfishness, contrasting with the ideal of living for God and goodness that Levin embraces in the last chapter. But for many readers, Anna's insistence on the dictates of her heart's desires makes her an unforgettable pioneer of the search for autonomy and passion in an alienating modern world.

KONSTANTIN LEVIN

Levin was originally a marginal character in the novel, but by the final version he had grown into its co-protagonist, as central as Anna herself. Levin is a veiled self-portrait of the author: his name includes Tolstoy's first name (Lev in Russian), and many of the details of his courtship of Kitty—including the missing shirt at the wedding—were taken straight from Tolstoy's life. Levin is thus a spokesman for Tolstoy's own views and desires, such as his dogged search for the meaning of life. Levin's confession of faith at the end of the novel straddles the line between art and morality—half fiction, half philosophy lesson—and parallels Tolstoy's turn to religion after writing *Anna Karenina*.

Independent-minded and socially awkward, Levin is a truly individual character who fits into none of the obvious classifications of Russian society. He is neither a freethinking rebel like his brother Nikolai, nor a bookish intellectual like his half-brother Sergei. He is not a socialite like Betsy, nor a bureaucrat like Karenin, nor a rogue like Veslovsky. Levin straddles the issue of Russia's fate as a western nation: he distrusts liberals who wish to westernize Russia, rejecting their analytical and abstract approach, but on the other hand he recognizes the utility of western technology and agricultural science. In short, Levin is his own person. He follows his own vision of things, even when it is confused and foggy, rather than adopting any group's prefabricated views. Moreover, Levin prefers isolation over fitting in with a social set with which he is not wholly comfortable. In this he resembles Anna, whose story is a counterpart to his own in its search for self-definition and individual happiness.

Despite his status as a loner, Levin is not self-centered, and he shows no signs of viewing himself as exceptional or superior. If Tolstoy makes Levin a hero in the novel, his heroism is not in his unique achievements but in his ability to savor common human experiences. His most unforgettable experiences in the novel—his bliss at being in love, his fear for his wife in childbirth—are not rare or aristocratic but shared by millions. Anyone can feel these emotions; Levin is special simply in feeling them so deeply and openly. This commonality gives him a humanitarian breadth that no other character in the novel displays. His comfort with his peasants and his loathing of social pretension characterize him as an ordinary man, one of the Russian people despite his aristocratic lineage. When Levin mows for an entire day alongside his peasants, we get no sense that he is deliberately slumming with the commoners—he sincerely enjoys the labor. Tolstoy's representation of Levin's final discovery of faith, which he learns from a peasant, is equally ordinary. In this regard, Levin incarnates the simple virtues of life and Tolstoy's vision of a model human being.

ALEXEI KARENIN

A government official with little personality of his own, Karenin maintains the façade of a cultivated and rational man. He keeps up with contemporary poetry, he reads books on Roman history for leisure, and he makes appearances at all the right parties. He is civil to everyone and makes no waves. Originally, Tolstoy conceived of Karenin as a saintly figure, a forgiving husband endlessly tormented by his wife's roving search for passion. But in the final version of the novel we feel the hollowness of Karenin's façade: he is less a saint than a bland bureaucrat whose personality has disappeared under years of devotion to his duties. He reads poetry but rarely has a poetic thought; he reads history but never reflects on it meaningfully. He does not enjoy himself or spark conversations at parties but merely makes himself seen and then leaves. Karenin's entire existence consists of professional obligations, with little room for personal whim or passion. When first made aware of Anna's liaison with Vronsky, Karenin briefly entertains thoughts of challenging Vronsky to a duel but quickly abandons the idea when he imagines a pistol pointed his direction. This cowardice is an indicator of his general resistance to a life of fervent emotion and grand passions.

Karenin's limp dispassion colors his home life and serves as the backdrop to Anna's rebellious search for love at any price. We feel that he must have viewed his betrothal to Anna as an act of duty like everything else in his life: it was time to marry, so he chose an appropriate girl who happened to be Anna. He never gives any indications of appreciating Anna's uniqueness or valuing the ways in which she differs from other women. His appreciation of her is only for her role as wife and mother. Similarly, Karenin's fatherly interaction with Seryozha is cold and official, focused on educational progress and never on Seryozha's perceptions or emotions. Karenin wishes to raise a responsible child, as he surely was himself. It is Karenin's obedience to duty, his pigeonholing of all persons and experiences as either appropriate or inappropriate, that Anna rejects. When Anna leaves, she does not simply dump Karenin the man but also the conventionalism that Karenin believes in and represents. Karenin's slide into occultism and stagnation at the end of the novel suggests indirectly how much he needed Anna, and how much she was the life behind his façade.

ALEXEI VRONSKY

In early drafts of the novel, Vronsky was a poetic hero, a dashing officer of great passion but little reliability. He was intended originally as a larger-than-life symbol of the Romantic values of independence, whim, and disobedience toward civilized society. In his final incarnation, Vronsky is a more moderate figure, less wildly rebellious and more socially conforming. He is still somewhat idealized: depicted as a handsome, wealthy, and charming person who is as willing as Anna is to abandon social standing and professional status in the pursuit of love. His commitment to his hospital-building project shows a Romantic passion for carrying out an individual vision of good. But despite his glories, Vronsky shows realistic faults and imperfections. His thinning hair, his error in judgment in the horse race, his thwarted ambitions of military glory all remind us that Vronsky is not a Romantic hero but a man like any other. He does not symbolize escape from social pressures, for he suffers from these pressures himself. He is an exceptional man, but he is only a man. This human limitation in Vronsky is Anna's greatest disappointment: we feel she yearned for a total escape into a dreamy love and that she simply cannot accept the reality of Vronsky's earthbound, limited passion. It is significant that Tolstoy gives Vronsky the same first name as Karenin, as if Anna's yearning for another Alexei only leads her to a disappointing repetition of her first one. Vronsky's inability to offer Anna a real alternative to conventional life may be the great tragedy of her later life.

Though we may feel a waning in Vronsky's devotion in the later chapters of the novel, we must be wary not to buy into Anna's paranoid fears too much. There is no sure indication that Vronsky loves Anna any less at the end. Certainly he cares for her more than ever: he outfits his country home with unheard-of luxury and elegance, largely (we feel) in an attempt to make Anna happy. His commissioning of Anna's portrait and his prominent display of it in their home suggests that he is still enraptured by her. Vronsky occasionally feels the pang of thwarted ambition, especially after meeting his school chum who is now highly successful, but this is only natural, and there is no sign he holds it against Anna. He bends over backward to accommodate her whims and endures her paranoid fits with patience. These actions may be mere solicitude—or "duty," as Anna calls it—on Vronsky's part, rather than true love. But since Tolstoy rarely shows us Vronsky's thoughts as he shows us Anna's, we simply cannot know for sure.

STIVA OBLONSKY

Stiva sets the novel in motion, not only in terms of plot—as the domestic upheaval caused by his infidelity brings Anna to Moscow, and thus to Vronsky—but also in terms of theme. Stiva embodies the notion that life is meant to be lived and enjoyed, not repressed by duties. He lives for the moment, thinking about responsibility only later, as his constant financial problems remind us. His dazed reaction to being chastised for adultery is not so much regret at his wrongdoing but rather regret at being caught. Indeed, even after Dolly forgives Stiva, he does not stop carrying on with other women. He does not feel any duty toward his wife and family that constrains his freedom.

Despite his actions, Stiva is not an objectionable character. His morality is so blithe and clueless, his belief that somehow he has a right to enjoy sex with whomever he pleases so sincere, that he almost converts us to his own pleasure-based philosophy. We may not go so far as to consider adultery justifiable, but at least we are led to ask questions about the relation between sexual pleasure and marital commitments, and between love and duty.

This questioning of love and duty sets the stage for Anna's much larger enactment of the same conflict between private passion and social obligation. Like Anna, Stiva cares little for the voices of conventional morality, preferring to seek out love and satisfaction in any way that is personally meaningful for him. But the similarity ends there. Stiva is far shallower than his sister, and lacks her emotional self-reflection and passionate intensity. His love affairs are trifles to him, whereas Anna's becomes a matter of life and death to her. Stiva is not a dynamic character in the novel—he does not change. He is never punished for his sins and never improves his behavior. In short, Stiva's constancy brings into relief the extraordinary changes—moral, spiritual, and psychological—that Anna undergoes.

THEMES, MOTIFS & SYMBOLS

THEMES

Themes are the fundamental and often universal ideas explored in a literary work.

SOCIAL CHANGE IN NINETEENTH-CENTURY RUSSIA

Tolstoy sets his tale of adultery and self-discovery against the backdrop of the huge historical changes sweeping through Russia during the late nineteenth century, making the historical aspects of the novel just as important as the personal and psychological aspects. In the Russia of *Anna Karenina,* a battle rages between the old patriarchal values sustaining the landowning aristocracy and the new, liberal—often called *"libre penseur,"* or freethinking, in the novel—values of the Westernizers. The old-timer conservatives believe in traditions like serfdom and authoritarian government, while the Westernizing liberals believe in technology, rationalism, and democracy. We see this clash in Levin's difficulty with his peasants, who, refusing to accept the Western agricultural innovations he tries to introduce, believe that the old Russian ways of farming are the best. We also see the confusion of these changing times in the question of the *zemstvo,* or village council, in which Levin tries to participate as a proponent of democracy but which he finally abandons on the grounds that they are useless.

The guests at Stiva's dinner party raise the question of women's rights—clearly a hot topic of the day, and one that shows the influence of Western social progress on Russia. That Dolly and Anna suffer in their marriages, however, does not bode well for the future of feminism in the world of the novel. Courtship procedures are equally uncertain in the world of *Anna Karenina.* The Russian tradition of arranged marriages is going out of fashion, but Princess Shcherbatskaya is horrified at the prospect of allowing Kitty to choose her own mate. The narrator goes so far as to say plainly that no one knows how young people are to get married in Russia in the 1870s. Taken together, all this confusion created by fading traditions creates an atmosphere of both instability and new potential, as if humans have to decide again how to live. It is only in such a changing atmosphere that Levin's philosophical questionings are possible.

THE BLESSINGS OF FAMILY LIFE

Tolstoy intended *Anna Karenina* to be a recognizable throwback to the genre of "family novels" popular in Russia several decades earlier, which were out of fashion by the 1870s. The Russian family novel portrayed the benefits and comforts of family togetherness and domestic bliss, often in a very idealized way. In the radically changing social climate of 1860s Russia, many social progressives attacked the institution of the family, calling it a backward and outmoded limitation on individual freedom. They claimed that the family often exploited children as cheap labor. Tolstoy wrote *Anna Karenina* in part as his personal statement on the family debate. The first sentence of the novel, concerning the happiness and unhappiness of families, underscores the centrality of this idea.

Tolstoy takes a pro-family position in the novel, but he is candid about the difficulties of family life. The notion that a family limits the freedom of the individual is evident in Stiva's dazed realization in the first pages of the novel that he cannot do whatever he pleases. This limitation of freedom is also evident in Levin's surprise at the fact that he cannot go off to visit his dying brother on a whim but must confer with his wife first and respond to her insistence that she accompany him. Yet despite these restrictions on personal liberty, and despite the quarrels that plague every family represented in *Anna Karenina*, Tolstoy portrays family life as a source of comfort, happiness, and philosophical transcendence. Anna destroys a family and dies in misery, whereas Levin creates a family and concludes the novel happily. Anna's life ultimately loses meaning, whereas Levin's attains it, as the last paragraph of the novel announces. Ultimately, Tolstoy leaves us with the conclusion that faith, happiness, and family life go hand in hand.

THE PHILOSOPHICAL VALUE OF FARMING

Readers of *Anna Karenina* are sometimes puzzled and frustrated by the extensive sections of the novel devoted to Levin's agricultural interests. We are treated to long passages describing the process of mowing, we hear much about peasant attitudes toward wooden and iron plows, and we are subjected to Levin's sociological theorizing about why European agricultural reforms do not work in Russia.

Yet this focus on agriculture and farming fulfills an important function in the novel and has a long literary tradition behind it. The idyll, a genre of literature dating from ancient times, portrays farmers and shepherds as more fulfilled and happy than their urban counterparts, showing closeness to the soil as a mark of the good life. Farmers understand growth and potential, and are aware of the delicate balance between personal labor and trust in the forces of nature. In *Anna Karenina*, Tolstoy updates the idyll by making his spokesman in the novel, Levin, a devoted farmer as well as an impassioned philosopher—and the only character in the novel who achieves a clear vision of faith and happiness.

For Levin, farming is a way of moving beyond oneself, pursuing something larger than one's own private desires—a pursuit that he sees as the cornerstone of all faith and happiness. His days spent mowing the fields bring him into closer contact with the Russian peasants—symbols of the native Russian spirit—than anyone else achieves. Other characters who harp on the virtues of peasants, such as Sergei, rarely interact with them. Levin's connections with farmers thus show him rooted in his nation and culture more so than Europeanized aristocrats like Anna. He is in closer touch with the truths of existence. It is no accident that Levin finally finds faith by listening to his peasant Fyodor, a farmer. Nor is it accidental that Levin's statement of the meaning of life in the novel's last paragraph recalls agriculture. Levin concludes that the value of life is in the goodness he puts into it—just as, we might say, the value of a farm lies in the good seeds and labor that the farmer puts into it. Ultimately, Levin reaches an idea of faith based on growth and cultivation.

MOTIFS

Motifs are recurring structures, contrasts, or literary devices that can help to develop and inform the text's major themes.

THE INTERIOR MONOLOGUE

Though Tolstoy has a reputation for being a simple and straightforward writer, he was in fact a great stylistic innovator. He pioneered the use of a device that is now commonplace in novels but was radically new in the nineteenth century—the interior monologue. The interior monologue is the author's portrayal of a character's thoughts and feelings directly, not merely in paraphrase or summary but as if directly issuing from the character's mind. Earlier writers such as Shakespeare had used the monologue in drama, writing scenes in which characters speak to the audience directly in asides or soliloquies. In narrative fiction, however, writers had rarely exploited the interior monologue for extended passages the way Tolstoy does in *Anna Karenina*. The interior monologue gives the reader great empathy with the character. When we accompany someone's thoughts, perceptions, and emotions step by step through an experience, we inevitably come to understand his or her motivations more intimately.

In *Anna Karenina*, Tolstoy gives us access to Levin's interior monologue at certain key moments in his life: his experience of the bliss of love when Kitty accepts him as husband, his physical ecstasy at mowing with the peasants, and his fear when Kitty is suffering in childbirth. But Tolstoy uses the device of interior monologue far more extensively and movingly in his portrayal of Anna's last moments, on her ride to the station where she dies at the end of Part Seven. Without access to her thoughts, we would have a much flimsier understanding of what drives Anna to suicide. Without it, her death would be just another casualty on the long list of women in Russian literature who kill themselves over love. Reading Anna's monologue, however, we see the liveliness and even humor that make her such a vivid individual in the novel, as when she interrupts her gloomy meditations to comment on the ridiculous name of the hairstylist Twitkin. We also see the extent to which Anna has become a burden to herself—she dreams of getting rid of Vronsky "and of myself." The interior monologue shows us her suicide not as a glamorous cliché but as a simple and heartbreaking attempt to rid herself of the very self she once attempted to liberate.

ADULTERY

Anna Karenina is best known as a novel about adultery: Anna's betrayal of her husband is the central event of its main plotline. There was a surge of interest in the topic of adultery in the mid-nineteenth century, as evidenced by works such as Nathaniel Hawthorne's *The Scarlet Letter* (1850) and Gustave Flaubert's *Madame Bovary* (1857). Although the guilty party in these works is always a woman who meets a bad end as a result of her wrongdoing, the nineteenth-century adultery novel is actually less religiously moralizing than we might expect. *Anna Karenina* is a case in point. Although the novel is loaded with biblical quotations issuing from the mouths of characters and from its own epigraph, its moral atmosphere is not overwhelmingly Christian. Indeed, many of the novel's devout Christian characters, such as Madame Stahl and Lydia Ivanovna, are repellent and hypocritical. Tolstoy rarely mentions the church in the novel, and even occasionally gently mocks it, as when Levin rolls his eyes at the confession he must undergo to get married. The religious stigma on adultery is certainly present but it is not all that strong.

The more important condemnation of adultery in *Anna Karenina* comes not from the church but from conventional society: adultery is more a social issue in the novel than a moral or religious one. Karenin's chief objection to Anna's involvement with Vronsky is not that adultery is a sin, or even that it causes him emotional anguish, but rather that society will react negatively. Karenin thinks of propriety and decency, looking good to the neighbors, over anything else. It is for this reason that he is so willing to overlook Anna's affair as long as she does not seek a separation or divorce. He does not care so much about the fact that his wife loves another man; he cares only that she continue to appear to be a good wife. This restrictive power of social convention is what Anna comes to loathe and tries to escape—first in Italy, then in seclusion in the countryside. As such, adultery in *Anna Karenina* is a side effect of the stifling forces of society, making the novel a work of social criticism as much as a story of marital betrayal.

FORGIVENESS

The idea of Christian forgiveness recurs regularly in *Anna Karenina* and is clearly one of Tolstoy's main topics of exploration in the novel. If the central action of the plot is a sin, then forgiveness is the potential resolution. And if Anna is a sinner, then our attitude toward her and toward the novel depends on whether and how much we can forgive her. Tolstoy establishes forgiveness as a noble ideal when Dolly exclaims to Anna, who is helping the Oblonskys through their marital difficulties, "If you forgive, it's completely, completely." This ideal form of pardon amounts to a total erasure of the sin "as if it hadn't happened," as Anna puts it. Yet Tolstoy does not mindlessly accept forgiveness as a noble Christian virtue, but instead forces us to consider whether forgiveness is possible and effective. The very epigraph to the novel—"Vengeance is mine; I will repay"—values vengeance, the opposite of forgiveness. This opening thought haunts the entire novel, suggesting that perhaps forgiveness is not the ultimate virtue after all.

Moreover, the characters' attitudes toward forgiveness are sometimes compromised. Dolly ends up forgiving Stiva, but we wonder whether her pardon amounts to her simply shutting her eyes to reality, as we know that Stiva continues his womanizing with unabated enthusiasm afterward. In Dolly's case, forgiveness looks like gullibility or resignation. Forgiveness is even more dubious in other instances. When the seemingly dying Anna begs Karenin's forgiveness and he grants it, both are sincere. But the forgiveness has little effect: Anna continues to love Vronsky and loathe Karenin as much as ever, and though Karenin is more amenable to the idea of divorce, his treatment of Anna does not change much. In another novel we might expect the Karenins or Oblonskys to renew their marital vows and live happily ever after, but for Tolstoy forgiveness does not have this fairy-tale effect. Karenin forgives Anna, but afterward their emotions remain the same as before. At the end of the novel, Anna begs forgiveness of God just before killing herself. Indirectly, she also begs it of us readers, for it is up to us to determine whether our emotional attraction to Anna outweighs our moral judgment of her life. Ultimately, for readers, forgiving her may be less important than identifying with her.

SYMBOLS

Symbols are objects, characters, figures, or colors used to represent abstract ideas or concepts.

TRAINS

In nineteenth-century western European novels, trains often appear as positive symbols of progress and technological advancement. In Russian literature, however, they have a more ambiguous meaning. Tolstoy saw the advent of the railroad as an insidious symbol of the spread of Western hyper-efficiency and rationalism in Russia, foreboding the end of easygoing native traditions. In this light, it is not surprising that the several references to trains in *Anna Karenina* all carry a negative meaning. Tolstoy sometimes has a character use the French word *train*, as when Anna complains about Vronsky's workload by saying *"Du train que cela va"*—at the rate his work is going—she will never see him at all in a few years. In this phrase, the word denotes a fast rate of increase of something harmful, which is exactly how Tolstoy viewed the expansion of the railroads.

Literal references to trains are no less negative. Anna first makes her ill-fated acquaintance with Vronsky in a train station, and she sees the death of a railway worker after this meeting as a bad omen.

The omen is fulfilled when Anna throws herself under the train near the end of the novel, literally making the railway her killer. The metaphor of transportation—and the "transports of love"—for a quick change of scenery is a clear one. Just as trains carry people away to new places, Anna herself is carried away by her train-station passion for Vronsky, which derails her family life, her social life, and ultimately her physical life as well.

VRONSKY'S RACEHORSE

On a literal level, Frou-Frou is the beautiful, pricey horse that Vronsky buys and then accidentally destroys at the officers' race. On a figurative level, Frou-Frou is a clear symbol of Anna, or of Vronsky's relationship with her—both of which are ultimately destroyed. Frou-Frou appears in the novel soon after Vronsky's affair with Anna becomes serious and dangerous for their social reputations. Vronsky meets Anna just before the race, and his conversation with her makes him nervous and unsettled, impairing his performance. This link connects Anna with Frou-Frou still more deeply, showing how Vronsky's liaison with Anna endangers him. The horse race is dangerous as well, as we find out when several officers and horses are injured during the run. Vronsky attempts to ride out both dangers—the horse race and the affair—with his characteristic coolness and poise, and he manages to do so successfully for a time. But his ability to stay on top of the situation is ultimately compromised by the fatal error he makes in sitting incorrectly on Frou-Frou's saddle, ending with a literal downfall for both man and horse.

The symbol of the racehorse implies much about the power dynamic between Anna and Vronsky. The horse is vulnerable and completely under Vronsky's control, just as in an adulterous affair in 1870s Russian society it is the woman who runs the greater risk of being harmed. For Vronsky and the other officer riders, the race is a form of entertainment in which they choose to participate. But there is a deeper force leading both Anna and Frou-Frou into the race, and the stakes are much higher for them than for Vronsky—the race is a matter of life and death for both woman and horse. Ultimately, the horse's death is a needless result of someone else's mistake, just as Anna's death seems unfair, a tragic waste of a beautiful life.

SYMBOLS

LEVIN AND KITTY'S MARRIAGE

Levin's courtship of and marriage to Kitty is of paramount importance to *Anna Karenina*. Tolstoy frames the marriage as a stubborn individualist's acceptance of and commitment to another human being, with all the philosophical and religious meaning such a connection carries for him. Levin is something of an outcast throughout the early part of the novel. His views alienate him from noblemen and peasantry alike. He is frustrated by Russian culture but unable to feel comfortable with European ways. He is socially awkward and suffers from an inferiority complex, as we see in his self-doubts in proposing to Kitty. Devastated by Kitty's rejection of his marriage proposal, Levin retreats to his country estate and renounces all dreams of family life. We wonder whether he will remain an eccentric isolationist for the rest of his days, without family or nearby friends, laboring over a theory of Russian agriculture that no one will read, as no one reads his brother Sergei's magnum opus.

When the flame of Levin's and Kitty's love suddenly rekindles, leading with lightning speed to a marriage, it represents more than a mere betrothal. Rather, the marriage is an affirmation of Levin's connection with others and his participation in something larger than himself—the cornerstone of the religious faith he attains after marriage. Levin starts thinking about faith when he is forced to go to confession in order to obtain a marriage license. Although he is cynical toward religious dogma, the questions the priest asks him set in motion a chain of thoughts that leads him through a crisis and then to spiritual regeneration. Similarly, Levin's final affirmation of faith on the last page of the novel is a direct result of his near-loss of the family that marriage has made possible. It is no accident that faith and marriage enter Levin's life almost simultaneously, for they are both affirmations that one's self is not the center of one's existence.

SUMMARY & ANALYSIS

PART ONE, CHAPTERS I–XVII

SUMMARY

All happy families are alike; each unhappy family is unhappy in its own way.

(See QUOTATIONS, p. 75)

Confusion reigns in the Oblonsky household in Moscow. Stiva Oblonsky has been unfaithful to his wife, Dolly, with their children's former governess. Stiva is distraught but not overly remorseful. Dolly, meanwhile, is devastated and refuses to leave her rooms. The servants advise Stiva to apologize repeatedly, predicting that Dolly will calm down. Stiva finally visits Dolly, begging her to remember their nine years of marriage. Dolly is inconsolable, telling her husband he is disgusting and a total stranger to her.

Stiva goes to his office. His job is respectable and comfortable, thanks to his charm and good connections. He receives a surprise visit from an old friend, Konstantin Levin, who lives in the country. Stiva introduces Levin to his business partners, saying that Levin is active in the *zemstvo*, his village administrative board. Levin reveals that he has quit his post on the board, and tells Stiva that he has an important matter to discuss. They arrange to meet for dinner. Stiva guesses the matter has something to do with his sister-in-law, Kitty Shcherbatskaya, with whom he knows Levin is in love.

While in Moscow, Levin stays with his half-brother, Koznyshev, whose philosophical mindset sometimes perplexes Levin. The brothers discuss Levin's plan to visit their estranged and sickly third brother, Nikolai, who is back in Moscow with a girlfriend. Koznyshev advises Levin not to go, saying Levin cannot help Nikolai, who wishes to be left alone.

Levin goes to the skating rink at the Zoological Gardens, where he is sure he will find the charming Kitty. She is at the rink, as expected. Levin and Kitty enjoy one another's company together on the ice until Levin confesses that he feels more confident whenever Kitty, a less accomplished skater, leans on him for support. Kitty's mood suddenly darkens, and she sends Levin away. Levin grows upset and goes off glumly to his dinner with Stiva.

Over the luxurious meal, Levin confesses to Stiva his passionate love for Kitty. Stiva encourages Levin to be hopeful but warns him of a rival for her affections, an officer named Alexei Vronsky. Stiva then discusses his own problematic infatuation with his children's governess. Levin gently chastises Stiva for his behavior, but Stiva laughingly calls Levin a moralist.

Kitty's mother, Princess Shcherbatskaya, weighs the relative merits of Vronsky and Levin as suitors. She is disconcerted by Levin's awkwardness and generally favors Vronsky. But the Princess is also aware that young Russian noblewomen of the new generation prefer to choose their husbands for themselves rather than submit to their parents' arrangements.

That evening, Levin calls at Kitty's home and finds her alone. Kitty is aware that she feels affection for him, but she loves Vronsky. She considers avoiding Levin entirely but then bravely meets him and declines his marriage proposal. Princess Shcherbatskaya is relieved to see that no engagement has been declared. Vronsky arrives, and the devastated Levin is impressed with this rival suitor. That night, Kitty cannot sleep, haunted by Levin's face. Kitty's father has learned about the rebuffed proposal and is upset, as he prefers Levin to Vronsky.

The next morning, Vronsky goes to the train station to meet his mother arriving from St. Petersburg. There he meets Stiva, who has come to meet his sister, Anna Karenina. Vronsky tells Stiva he has met Levin, whom he finds nice but somewhat awkward. Stiva defends Levin, hinting that Levin might have proposed to Kitty. Vronsky states that Kitty can find a better match. Meanwhile the train arrives, and Vronsky awaits his mother.

ANALYSIS

Although *Anna Karenina* is renowned as a study of romantic passion, the novel shows us the dark and discouraging side of romance from the first page. Tolstoy's novel begins when the honeymoon is already over. Deception and disappointment mar the marriage of Stiva and Dolly, two attractive, rich, cultured, sensitive, and likable people. We expect them to be the ideal happy couple, but they are miserable, and the source of the problem is their marriage. Tolstoy's crafty decision to open the novel with the threat of a marital breakup casts a dark shadow over all the love and romance in *Anna Karenina*. As much as we may later want to believe in Vronsky's passion for Anna, in the back of our minds lingers a bleak memory of this opening scene and of the formidable problems facing all romantic couples. Tolstoy extends this dark shadow over many romantic moments in the novel. For example, Levin and Kitty's turn at the skating rink is almost a stereotypical portrayal of dreamy-eyed lovers, but Tolstoy kills the romance by having Kitty rebuff Levin's forwardness. Love seems doomed from the start.

Stiva is a crucial character because he is, in many ways, an advance introduction to his sister, Anna Karenina. His adultery opens the novel; her later adultery is the novel's main focus. Moreover, they share personality traits and moral attitudes. For one thing, there is an inexplicable aura of innocence around Stiva. He has made mistakes but is far from a villain. Because Tolstoy presents Stiva as such an affable and sincere character, it is nearly impossible even for the most moralistic of us to condemn Stiva wholeheartedly, even if we disapprove of his adulterous liaisons. Despite his lack of restraint, he is not a bad man, and is even quite charming. His flaw is not willful cruelty or meanness but simply his "amorous" nature, as Tolstoy euphemistically puts it. Stiva likes sexual adventure, and in his mind it is not wrong. He regrets not having hidden the affair more thoroughly but does not regret the affair itself, which brought him pleasure, as he openly admits. The question of a right to sexual pleasure is further examined later, in his sister Anna's situation.

Though *Anna Karenina* is on the surface a novel about romantic love and courtship, it is actually far more wide-ranging in its focus, delving into public and social topics such as technology, agriculture, and administration. Tolstoy's explorations of social themes strike many readers as annoying interruptions of the love story, but in fact the novel's social concerns and its love theme often reinforce each other. The train, for example, is a symbol of modernization and European efficiency. But it is also recurrently associated with Anna and her "transport" of passion upon meeting Vronsky. Anna appears in the novel near a train, and thrillingly meditates on Vronsky as she rides the train to St. Petersburg. Perhaps most important, a train is involved in Anna's final fate at the end of the novel. The train, like Anna's adultery, is for Tolstoy an unfortunate product of the modern world. The novel's social themes intersect with its romantic themes again in the discussion of the Shcherbatskys' confusion about Kitty's courtship. It is no longer possible for Russian parents to arrange marriages, but at the same time, children like Kitty cannot choose for themselves. The result is that no one knows how to proceed, and the risks seem huge. Modernization may improve the quality of Russian life, but it also disrupts the fabric of Russian society and courtship.

PART ONE, CHAPTERS XVIII–XXXIV

SUMMARY

It was as if a surplus of something so overflowed her being that it expressed itself beyond her will, now in the brightness of her glance, now in her smile.

(See QUOTATIONS, p. 76)

Vronsky waits for his mother at the train station. Before she appears, Vronsky sees a woman with gentle, shining gray eyes whose face becomes animated at the sight of him. This is Anna Karenina, whom Stiva has come to the station to meet. Anna and Vronsky briefly exchange glances. Vronsky's mother appears and introduces Vronsky to Anna. As they are leaving the station, a worker is run over by a train and killed—whether it is suicide or an accident is unclear. Anna gloomily views the death as a bad omen.

Stiva takes Anna to his home, where Dolly, devastated by grief over her husband's adultery, wishes to see no one. But Anna, having heard about the betrayal, insists on seeing Dolly and meets her warmly and compassionately. She does not attempt to console Dolly but is deeply sympathetic. She tells Dolly that Stiva is suffering and that he is capable of total repentance. Dolly feels much better.

Later that day, Kitty arrives at the Oblonsky residence, and Anna receives her warmly. Anna hears about Kitty's interest in Vronsky, and says she met Vronsky at the station and liked him. At teatime, Dolly emerges from her rooms, and Kitty and Anna understand that Dolly and Stiva have been reconciled. They discuss the upcoming ball, and Kitty urges Anna to wear a lilac-colored dress. Later, Vronsky stops by the Oblonsky household and seems ashamed when he sees Anna.

At the ball held not long afterward, Vronsky dances the first dance with Kitty, who looks radiant. Anna appears, dressed not in lilac but in black, which Kitty immediately realizes is Anna's best color. Kitty is puzzled by Anna's refusal to respond when Vronsky bows to her. Kitty dances many waltzes with Vronsky but later finds Anna and Vronsky dancing together. Anna looks elated and triumphant. For the final mazurka, Kitty turns away her suitors, expecting Vronsky to ask her to dance. She is stunned to see that Vronsky has spurned her to dance the last dance with Anna.

Meanwhile, Levin gloomily reflects on his life after Kitty's rejection. He decides to pay a visit to his brother Nikolai. Upon arriving, Levin finds his sickly brother much thinner than he remembered. Nikolai introduces Levin to his companion, Marya Nikolaevna, whom he saved from a whorehouse. Over dinner, Nikolai speaks at length about his socialist views. Marya privately tells Levin that Nikolai drinks too much. Levin leaves, having made Mary promise to write to him in case of need. Levin returns to his country estate, grateful for the blessings of his peaceful existence.

At the Oblonskys', Anna and Dolly dine together by themselves. Anna is unwell, and Kitty sends word that she has a headache. Anna expresses her amazement at having danced with Vronsky. She is confident that Vronsky will still pursue Kitty, but Dolly is not so sure. Anna leaves for St. Petersburg, relieved to escape Vronsky. On the train she is tormented by self-doubt, unsure of who she is. As the train pauses at a station, Anna glimpses Vronsky on the platform and feels a joyful pride. He has followed her from Moscow.

Arriving in St. Petersburg, Anna meets her husband, Karenin, at the station. Vronsky watches them together and can see that Anna does not love Karenin. Anna introduces the two men, and Vronsky asks if he may call at the Karenin home. At home, Anna's son, Seryozha, runs up to greet her, and Anna feels a sudden pang of disappointment in her son. She speaks to her morally upright friend Lydia Ivanovna and feels secure that nothing scandalous has happened in her relations with Vronsky. Anna dismisses her anxieties.

While in St. Petersburg, Vronsky socializes with his colleague Petritsky, to whom he has lent his apartment, and Petritsky's lady friend, Baroness Shilton. They lightheartedly chat before Vronsky leaves to make appearances at various places where he hopes to encounter Anna.

ANALYSIS

In his depiction of Anna's appearance at the train station during her first meeting with Vronsky, Tolstoy emphasizes Anna's spiritual rather than physical attributes. This method of characterizing her is important, for it reinforces the intellectual and philosophical aspect of this novel of ideas. While Anna and Vronsky are clearly attracted to each other, their mutual interest is more abstract than bodily, more about attractiveness of personality and manner than about sexual fantasy. Though Anna's figure is ravishing, Vronsky is drawn primarily to her "gentle and tender" eyes. Her eyes are not a sultry brown or coquettish blue but rather a subtle gray, the same color as the eyes of Athena, Greek goddess of wisdom—hardly a symbol of unbridled passion. (Although Tolstoy may also have had in mind Shakespeare's writing, in which gray eyes represent the paragon of female beauty.) At the ball, Anna appears not in the archetypal red of a femme fatale but rather in a stunning but tasteful black dress. These clues tell us from the very beginning that although Tolstoy may harshly condemn adultery on an abstract level, he does not portray Anna as a passion-crazed vixen—as popular novels of the time often represented the straying wife.

Anna's appearance also reinforces the importance of family life in the novel. Anna is not a vamp who thwarts old-fashioned Russian family values or shows hostility to domestic harmony. On the contrary, her initial appearance in Moscow—and in the novel—is prompted by her desire to see a family stay together. Anna's mission to reconcile her brother and his wife is successful; she brings a couple on the verge of separation back together. Anna is also naturally motherly: in her conversations with Dolly's children, she shows that she is aware of their individual personalities almost as much as their own mother is. Moreover, Anna is clearly devoted to her own eight-year-old son, Seryozha, from whom she is apart for the first time in his life when she goes to Moscow. Even more important, Anna has no bone to pick with society's expectations of propriety. She does not willfully flout public norms of behavior. When she finds herself dancing with Vronsky, she is startled by her own actions.

The parallel structure of Anna's and Levin's story lines—one of Tolstoy's strokes of genius in composing *Anna Karenina*—allows us to make subtle and continuous comparisons and contrasts between the two characters and their fates. On the most obvious level, their stories begin on very different notes: Anna finds love with Vronsky just at the moment when Levin loses love with Kitty. Anna's decision to act on her feelings brings her thrills and excitement, whereas Levin's decision brings him dejection and depression. These contrasts, however, only point out how similar the two characters are. Both Anna and Levin seek truth in their personal relationships, unwilling to settle for anything less. Anna discovers that she would prefer to suffer with her true love rather than continue to lead a life of lies and deceit with a man she does not love deeply. Anna's unconventional actions are prompted by a desire not for rebellion for its own sake but for absolute sincerity in her emotional life. Similarly, Levin, after Kitty's rebuff, does not go after the next girl on his list but resigns himself to eternal bachelorhood and withdraws to the country. Like Anna, Levin wants all or nothing in love.

PART TWO, CHAPTERS I–XVII

SUMMARY

The Shcherbatskys are concerned about Kitty's health, which has been failing ever since the ball at which Vronsky slighted her. Though secretly convinced that love is the cause of Kitty's ill health, the Shcherbatskys consult numerous doctors. Dolly attempts to talk with Kitty about her feelings. Kitty is initially resistant but then breaks down in tears. Dolly intuits that Kitty has rejected Levin only to be forsaken by Vronsky, and that the pain of this turn of events has devastated her.

Anna frequents a different social circle now, preferring the company of Vronsky's worldly cousin Betsy Tverskoy to that of her former companion, the morally righteous Lydia Ivanovna. At a party, rumors about Anna's liaison with Vronsky spread, and Anna falls prey to some vicious gossipers, though others defend her.

Anna and Vronsky meet at Betsy's. Anna begs Vronsky to drop their relationship and ask for Kitty's forgiveness. Vronsky affirms his hope for happiness with Anna, as her eyes assure him that she loves him. Karenin enters but soon leaves, while Anna decides to stay at Betsy's for supper. At home Karenin meditates on his feeling that something is amiss. He feels jealous, though he knows jealousy is illogical. When he tries to picture Anna's personal life to himself, he becomes confused and uncomfortable.

When Anna arrives home from Betsy's, her husband confronts her, warning her about the risks of her behavior. Anna becomes mildly indignant, affirming her right to a little merriment. Karenin states that some things should lie hidden in one's soul, implying that Anna's attraction to Vronsky is one such thing. Karenin tells Anna he loves her, but she wonders what this means. She tells him she wants to go to bed, and withdraws.

The narrative skips forward almost a year, to the point at which Anna and Vronsky have finally consummated their affair. After the deed is done, Anna sobs, saying that all she has now is Vronsky. She tries to drive away her thoughts. Sleeping, she dreams that both Karenin and Vronsky are her husbands.

Meanwhile, Levin's sadness about Kitty's rejection lingers. He busies himself with farm planning on his estate and sends his brother Nikolai, who suffers from tuberculosis, off to a spa in Europe for treatment. Levin feels frustrated with his farm work and with the stubbornness and stupidity of his peasant workers.

When the bell rings one day, Levin wonders whether his brother Nikolai has come for a visit. He is pleased to see that it is Stiva Oblonsky. Levin, grateful for a potential source of information about Kitty, takes Stiva out to hunt birds. Unexpectedly, Levin blurts out a question about Kitty, unable to restrain his curiosity. When Stiva replies that Kitty is ill, Levin is oddly pleased, thinking that he has had an effect on her.

On the way home, Levin and Stiva discuss a forest that Stiva plans to sell. Levin claims the deal is shady and accuses the merchant buyer of intending to cheat Stiva. Visiting the merchant along with Stiva, Levin refuses to shake the merchant's hand. Stiva makes the sale anyway, and later playfully accuses Levin of snobbery.

ANALYSIS

In these chapters we see a number of characters who recognize, or deny, their feelings. Emotional self-knowledge becomes a crucial theme. Anna and Levin are at one end of the emotional spectrum, acknowledging what they feel and accepting the troubling conse- quences that accompany their feelings, come what may. Other char- acters, however, are less able to admit their inner emotions to themselves or to others. Kitty, with her evasive and roundabout atti- tude toward Levin, serves as a direct contrast to Anna and her unquestioning acceptance of her feelings for Vronsky. The image of Levin haunts Kitty both while he courts her and after she rejects him, but all the while she is unable to admit to herself that she cares for him. Kitty's alleged illness is a clear cover-up for and result of her emotional pain. She thinks she feels humiliation when in fact she feels a deep affection that reveals itself as *Anna Karenina* unfolds. Kitty's conversation with Dolly, in which Kitty breaks down in tears on the subject of Levin, marks one stage in Kitty's gradual acceptance of her feelings. For Kitty, this is a slow process. The difference is striking: Anna acknowledges her love for Vronsky in a matter of days, whereas Kitty takes years to accept her feelings for Levin.

Karenin contrasts even more extremely with Anna's and Levin's emotional self-honesty. Whereas Kitty stifles her feelings, Karenin locks them away entirely, even going so far as to reject the very idea of emotional truth. After Anna returns home from Betsy's, Karenin, in reference to Anna's fantasies about Vronsky, tells her that some things in a person's soul are best kept hidden. This word choice is revealing: Karenin does not mind that his wife may have feelings for another man—he only objects to her acting on them in a way that other people can see. For Karenin, repression is a way of life: he has kept his feelings so quarantined that his approach to life and love is wholly, coldly rational. When coming to terms with his jealousy of Vronsky, Karenin does not succumb to passion or violence but tries to convince himself that jealousy is "illogical," as if his troubles with Anna were a math problem rather than a deeply personal matter. This dry, analytical approach defines not only Karenin's relationship to his wife but also his profession and attitude toward his work. Much like his character Levin, Tolstoy hated bureaucrats such as Karenin, rejecting their way of transforming the whole of life into equations, rules, and quotas. For Tolstoy, such cold rationality was anti-Russian. He believed that those like Karenin presented not merely romantic failure but a social threat as well.

The most crucial plot event in the novel—the consummation of Anna's and Vronsky's love—passes almost unnoticed. Whether Tolstoy chose to leave this love scene undeveloped for reasons of censorship or artistry, the event is marked only by an ellipsis between Chapters X and XI. Whatever the reason, this omission forces us to see that titillation is not Tolstoy's aim in writing the novel. *Anna Karenina* is a novel of ideas much more than a tale of lust. As such, it focuses on the thoughts and feelings this love affair elicits rather than on what actually happens in the bedroom. The bleakness of Chapter XI, the scene immediately after the affair begins, highlights how far from sexy the situation is. Vronsky's seduction of Anna is marked by sadness rather than happiness, contrary to all our expectations. Anna is not joyful but grieving, sobbing and declaring that she has lost everything—right at the moment when she gets everything she has wanted. Anna's emotions are those of a jilted lover, not a fulfilled one. We realize what a tragic figure Anna is and see that her love is marked not by pleasure but by desperation.

PART TWO, CHAPTERS XVIII–XXXIV

SUMMARY
Vronsky continues life as usual in his regiment. Though he never lets slip that he loves Anna, the whole of St. Petersburg high society knows about his feelings for her. The women who once praised Anna as righteous now wait for a chance to sling mud in her face.

Vronsky hears about an upcoming officers' steeplechase, so he buys a new mare, named Frou-Frou, to ride in one of the races. On the day of the races, Vronsky visits Frou-Frou in the stable, and she grows more agitated as he approaches. Vronsky reflects on everyone pestering him about Anna.

Just before the horse race, Vronsky visits Anna at her nearby summer house. She has been thinking about him and seems somewhat distraught. Her son, Seryozha, is absent, as Vronsky had hoped. Anna informs Vronsky that she is pregnant. He urges her to leave her husband and live with him instead. Vronsky cannot imagine how Anna can wish to continue living in such deceit, not realizing that the reason is her love for her son. Suddenly, Vronsky realizes he is late for the races.

Vronsky arrives at the racetrack just as Frou-Frou is being led out of the stable. Vronsky's brother, Alexander, approaches him and tells him to answer a letter their mother has recently sent. Vronsky is expected to do well in the race, as his only serious rival is another officer, Makhotin, who rides a horse named Gladiator. Nonetheless, Vronsky is agitated. The race begins. After a slow start, Frou-Frou outpaces all the horses except Gladiator. At last, Frou-Frou pulls ahead of Gladiator, and is in the lead. Vronsky is ecstatic. But during a jump over a ditch, he shifts in the saddle incorrectly, causing Frou-Frou to fall. The horse breaks her back and must be shot.

Meanwhile, the Karenins' relationship, on the surface, has remains just the same as before. Unable to face or admit his own feelings for his wife, Karenin treats Anna with an offended hostility. He hardly ever sees her, as she goes away for the summer, living near Betsy Tverskoy's home in the countryside. At the officers' steeplechase, which Anna and Betsy attend together, Karenin observes that his wife only has eyes for Vronsky. When Vronsky falls, Anna weeps with alarm, and then with relief after hearing that he is safe. Karenin offers to take Anna home, but she prefers to stay. Karenin tells Anna that her visible grief upon Vronsky's fall is highly improper. Finally, on the carriage ride home, Anna frankly confesses to Karenin that she loves Vronsky and hates Karenin. The shocked Karenin demands that she continue to observe the outward conventions of marriage for appearances' sake until a suitable solution is found.

Meanwhile, Kitty and some of her family are at a spa in Germany. The Shcherbatskys enjoy socializing with European aristocrats as they await an improvement in Kitty's health. One of the spa guests is a snobby, elderly, Russian invalid named Madame Stahl, who is famously devout and is accompanied by a young girl named Varenka. Kitty likes Varenka immensely but is nervous about meeting her. Kitty's mother learns that two spa guests, a tattered Russian gentleman and his female companion, are in fact Levin's brother Nikolai and Nikolai's girlfriend. One day, Kitty's mother is so impressed with Varenka that she allows Kitty to meet the girl. Kitty is delighted, and both mother and daughter are enchanted by Varenka's goodness.

Following Varenka's example of charity, Kitty throws herself into devotion and good deeds. She befriends a sad painter named Petrov, visiting him often. However, Petrov's wife eventually becomes jealous of Kitty, who is upset that her good intentions have gone astray. Near the end of Kitty's treatment, her father, Prince Shcherbatsky, returns from his travels elsewhere in Germany. He entertains his family and various others at the spa with his easy manner and funny jokes. The Prince chats with Madame Stahl, who he claims is bedridden not from illness but from vanity, merely because her legs are stubby. Her idealized, pious image of Madame Stahl deflated, Kitty never sees the old woman in the same way again.

━━━━━━━━━━━━

ANALYSIS

One of Tolstoy's main concerns in *Anna Karenina* is the conflict between inner and outer life, between private passions and the public social conventions that bind those passions. We see this tension in Karenin's reaction to the news of Anna's adultery. Unlike Anna, Karenin has no expectation that outward appearances should match the heart's inner feelings—he is content to live with a glaring disparity between the two. He tells Anna that she must maintain the status quo until he finds a suitable solution, which effectively means living the same life of deceit and lies with which Anna has struggled prior to her confession. Karenin's position ensures that Anna's admission of adultery changes nothing. Nothing changes later, either, when Karenin insists on formally maintaining his marriage. Although Anna has done wrong, she at least is aligned with the side of truth. In contrast, Karenin, who technically has done no wrong, is guilty in the sense that he prefers falsity just for the sake of maintaining appearances.

Vronsky's disaster in the horse race is a brilliant symbol of the difficulties he faces as Anna's lover. Tolstoy fills the scene with implicit comparisons between the horses' obstacle course and the love affair. Vronsky is on public display as he rides in the officers' steeplechase, just as his love affair with Anna is on public display despite all his efforts to keep it secret. He struggles to control Frou-Frou, a creature he does not know well, just as he struggles to understand the still-unfamiliar intricacies of his relationship with Anna. Moreover, much like a romantic relationship, Vronsky's relationship with his horse is more of a partnership than a situation of mastery and submission. He cannot rule the horse completely but can only hope for the best. Frou-Frou and Vronsky seem to have a strong rapport, but the horse grows increasingly nervous as Vronsky approaches her just before the race—just as the relationship between Vronsky and Anna becomes more unsettled as the lovers grow closer. Vronsky's troubling conversations with Anna and his brother before the race impair his concentration and his ability to ride, emphasizing still further the connection between his horse race and his relationship. In light of these parallels, the race is darkly prophetic. Vronsky's false move on the saddle, which inadvertently breaks Frou-Frou's back and leads to her death, foreshadows Vronsky's unintentional yet disastrous wounding of Anna.

Kitty's involvement with Varenka and Madame Stahl demonstrates Tolstoy's ability to approach the central themes and concerns of *Anna Karenina* from various angles, so subtly that we are hardly conscious of it. Kitty's stay at the German spa offers a parallel tale of a character swept away by illusions and then rudely awakened to disillusionment. Tolstoy presents Kitty's disenchantment with Madame Stahl in a way that makes us think twice about Anna's infatuation with Vronsky. When Kitty becomes enamored with Varenka and Madame Stahl, she is gloriously happy to have found a higher aim for her life, a transcendent vision of charity and piety to lift her up. But as Kitty's father points out to her later, Madame Stahl is less an invalid angel of virtue and goodness than a vain woman who stays in bed because her legs are stubby. In imitating Madame Stahl, Kitty performs acts of goodness that are not sincere, as she herself admits eventually. Indeed, Kitty causes more harm than good when she makes Petrov's wife jealous and upset. In presenting this sequence of infatuation and disillusionment, Tolstoy implies that Anna may be in love with an illusion as well, causing unnecessary harm to those around her. We see what Anna may not yet see: Vronsky is not a Prince Charming but rather an ordinary man with the same limitations as everyone else, including Anna's own husband.

Part Three, Chapters I–XVIII

Summary

Levin's half-brother, Sergei Koznyshev, takes a break from his intellectual work by visiting Levin at his country estate. Whereas Koznyshev sees the countryside as a place of leisure, Levin sees it as a place of hard labor. The brothers also have different attitudes toward the peasantry: Koznyshev is naïvely affectionate, whereas Levin has a close familiarity with the peasants that makes him occasionally critical. But if one were to ask Levin whether or not he loved the peasantry, he would be unable to answer.

On his walks with Levin in the country, Koznyshev waxes lyrical about the beauty of nature, while Levin prefers simply to look at his surroundings without comment. The men discuss the *zemstvo* board and the sad state of local affairs. Koznyshev wonders why nothing good comes from the money landowners pay to local bureaucrats, as there are no schools, doctors, or midwives to show for these payments. He chastises Levin for withdrawing from the *zemstvo*, where he might have exerted a positive impact. Levin asserts that such bureaucratic work was futile and frustrating for him. The next day, Levin works through his troubles by doing hard labor, mowing his fields alongside forty-two peasant men. The work exhilarates him, and he feels a higher force moving his scythe. Back home, Koznyshev hands Levin a letter from Dolly, in which she writes that she is at her nearby estate of Yergushovo.

Dolly has moved to the country to reduce household expenses, but she finds the hardships of rural life almost unbearable. Only with the help of the nanny, Matryona, is Dolly able to set up house decently. One day, Levin visits Dolly, who eagerly broaches the subject of Kitty. Levin reveals that he had proposed to Kitty and been refused. Contrary to Levin's assumption, Dolly did not already know about his rejected proposal. Dolly affirms that Kitty is suffering even more than Levin. Dolly attempts to talk about the future of a relationship between Levin and Kitty, but Levin gets angry, saying that such possibilities are dead forever.

The next day, Levin inspects his hay reserves, finding that the peasants have been cheating him of a considerable portion of his income, although they all cheerfully deny his claim. Despite this annoyance, Levin feels that the countryside is where he belongs and that he is not destined to marry. But when he glimpses Kitty passing by him in a carriage one day, his love for her suddenly returns.

Karenin sticks to his routine doggedly after Anna's revelation of her adultery, attempting to live as if nothing has changed. Inwardly, however, the pain he feels and represses leads him to curse Anna as a "depraved woman." He also grows more distant and cold toward his son, Seryozha. Karenin recites to himself the long list of men whom women have ruined over the course of history, from ancient to modern times. He considers challenging Vronsky to a duel but rejects the idea out of fear of pistols. Karenin reasons that the best punishment for Anna is to keep her bound to him, unable to divorce. He writes a letter to her explaining this plan to her formally.

Anna is utterly surprised by Karenin's decision, disappointed that the divorce for which she yearns will not come to pass. She is enraged at the prospect of prolonging her life of lies with Karenin. She writes a letter to him, telling him she is leaving the house and taking her son with her, but in the end she does not send the letter.

At a party at Betsy's, Anna talks to some young members of the fashionable St. Petersburg set and is struck by how bored they are despite their merry lives. One of the party guests, Liza, asks how happy one can be lolling around on a sofa all day.

ANALYSIS

Though Levin's extended meditations on farming may at first appear to be a digression away from the primary concerns of the novel, this focus on agriculture, much like Kitty's experiences at the spa, leads us toward questions that are relevant to Anna's story. Levin struggles with the dilemma of how to establish a sustainable relationship with the natural world, which he finds beautiful, rich, and giving, and which he loves dearly. His love for the countryside is evident from the bliss he experiences in mowing all day. Yet Levin realizes that bliss is not enough, and that his relation to nature is threatened on all sides by others, including the peasants who mistrust him and the westernized agricultural theorists who counsel fruitless so-called improvements. Levin tries hard to practice good husbandry but always seems to fail. Levin's problems with his land have elements in common with Anna and Vronsky's predicament. Anna and Vronsky's love is true and natural, and their early spiritual delight in each other is comparable to Levin's feeling of rapture and fulfillment when mowing. Yet we see that, like Levin, Vronsky and Anna have trouble managing this love that should be so simple and natural but that society resists from all sides. The central question in both situations is whether society can ever learn to accommodate nature—whether grain fields or love—without loss or sacrifice.

It is symbolically important that Dolly suddenly appears in the countryside after being associated with the city up to this point in the novel. For Levin, Dolly is a sort of stand-in for her sister, Kitty. Levin was once in love with Dolly too, as well as with the rest of the Shcherbatsky family. We learn that Levin viewed the Shcherbatsky girls as goddesses or dreams fleetingly descending to greet him. After Kitty rejects Levin, he keeps her on her dreamy pedestal as an untouchable figure. But when Dolly moves to the more rugged Russian countryside—where she can no longer be an idealized dream but must deal with daily hardships—she brings the Shcherbatskys down to earth for Levin. Dolly represents a hope that the two things Levin loves most, Kitty and the countryside, may be united. While Levin still outwardly insists that his relationship with Kitty is over, we feel that the flame of his love for her still burns. Ideal life and real life may join for Levin eventually.

Tolstoy's representation of Karenin changes gradually but drastically, so that by this point in the novel we are likely to have a very different image of him from the image we had earlier, without fully realizing that our perception of him has altered. Karenin is a competent but colorless statesman: a perfectly nice person but too absorbed in policy decisions and abstract issues to develop much of a distinct personality. Tolstoy initially depicts Karenin in neutral situations, with characters referring to his public role as one of the most important men in St. Petersburg. But at this point in the novel, Tolstoy reveals more of Karenin's feelings, which do not enhance our respect for him. Karenin believes himself to be rational, but when he thinks of Anna as a "depraved woman," we feel he exaggerates irrationally. Similarly, when Karenin reviews the list of men whom women have wronged throughout history, he comes across as pretentious and comical, just as he does when he rejects the idea of a duel because he is scared of pistols. Our regard for Karenin sinks, just as Anna's regard for him does. This shift is precisely Tolstoy's intention, making us feel as if we evolve along with the heroine of the novel.

PART THREE, CHAPTERS XIX–XXXII

SUMMARY

Vronsky brings his financial accounts into balance. Despite rumors of his huge fortune, he actually leads a hand-to-mouth existence. However, he adheres to a rule he imposed on himself long before and refuses to ask his mother for a loan. Vronsky obeys his rules of conduct rigorously, and it is only with the recent appearance of Anna in his life that he has felt conflicted about proper behavior.

Upon learning of Anna's pregnancy, Vronsky feels that he should resign from military service. He is reluctant to give up his professional ambitions, however, especially because his old school friend—and friendly rival—Serpukhovskoy has recently found fame. Serpukhovskoy warns Vronsky to be wary of women, as they can hold a man back from his full career potential.

Vronsky sets off for Anna's country house, where she has arranged a meeting with him. On the way, he feels he loves her more than ever, and his pulse quickens upon his first glimpse of her. Anna reveals to Vronsky that she has told her husband about their adulterous affair. Vronsky fears a duel, but after reading Karenin's letter to Anna he does not know how to react. Vronsky thinks about Serpukhovskoy's advice to him but knows he cannot tell Anna about it. He advises Anna to abandon Seryozha, her son with Karenin, and put an end to the humiliating situation by obtaining a divorce. Anna bursts out sobbing, saying that she is not humiliated but proud.

Karenin delivers a speech before the commission on the relocation of the Russian native tribes, and it is a brilliant success. Anna goes to her home in St. Petersburg to talk with her husband. She reaffirms to him that she is the one at fault but says that she cannot change anything. Karenin, exclusively concerned about defending his honor, makes only one demand—that Vronsky never set foot in his home. Anna and Karenin part.

Meanwhile, Levin has come to loathe the farm work he once enjoyed. He feels worn down from his unending struggle with the peasants over their reluctance to adopt new technological innovations for farming. More tormenting is the nearby presence of Kitty at Yergushovo; Levin yearns to see her but feels he cannot. Dolly tries to lure Levin to visit—and encounter Kitty—by requesting to borrow a saddle from him. Levin merely sends the saddle by courier, without visiting Dolly's house personally.

The torture of being near Kitty but not with her eventually becomes unbearable, so Levin takes off to visit his friend Sviyazhsky, who lives far away. On the way, Levin stops to eat at the home of a prosperous peasant. The peasant and his healthy family impress Levin, as does the farmer's obvious financial success. The old farmer asserts that landowners cannot rely on hired men, for peasants handle a farm best on their own.

At Sviyazhsky's house, Levin's host seems intent on arranging a marriage between Levin and his sister-in-law. Levin does his best to avoid talking to the sister-in-law, knowing in his heart that he can marry only Kitty or no one at all.

At dinner, Sviyazhsky entertains two old-fashioned landowners who miss the bygone days of serfdom in Russia. One of the landowners claims that farming was better in those days, and that the emancipation of the serfs has ruined Russia. Levin meditates on the fact that, in virtually all aspects of Sviyazhsky's life, there are huge contradictions between what Sviyazhsky inwardly believes and what he outwardly lives.

Sviyazhsky argues that all farming should be done under a rational, scientific system, whereas one of the landowner guests asserts that farming simply requires a firm authority looming over the peasantry. Levin agrees that his attempts to introduce farming innovations to the peasants have been disastrous. Sviyazhsky maintains that serfdom is a thing of the past and that hired labor is the future that all Russian landowners must accept. He asserts that education is the key to winning over the peasants, but Levin disagrees. Thinking about the matter afterward, Levin believes the answer is to treat the peasants not as an abstract workforce but as specifically *Russian* peasants whose specific traditions and nature must be factored into all decisions involving labor. Levin is determined to put his new theory into practice on his estate, making the peasants financial partners in the harvest. The peasants resist, however, suspecting Levin of somehow trying to cheat them.

As Levin makes plans to visit farms in western Europe to research his new agricultural theory, his brother Nikolai visits. Nikolai, who is even sicker than before, has abandoned Marya Nikolaevna. Since only one room in the house is heated, Levin allows Nikolai to sleep in his own bedroom. Nikolai's incessant coughing and cursing keep Levin awake all hours of the night. With his brother obviously dying, Levin can think of nothing but death. He gets up to examine his graying temples, affirming that he has a few good years left in his life. He goes back to bed wondering whether there is anything he can do to help his brother.

The next day, conversation between the brothers is strained, as the despairing and self-pitying Nikolai purposely irritates Levin by mocking his ideas about agricultural improvement. Nikolai leaves but at the last minute asks for Levin's forgiveness. Levin later meets a friend, to whom he speaks about death. Levin is aware that he must live out his life to the end, come what may.

ANALYSIS

In this portion of the novel, Tolstoy shows us some of the unexpected and seemingly contradictory aspects of Vronsky's character. Though Vronsky's methodical accounting practices appear to be at odds with his devil-may-care image, we see that they are as integral to his character as his wild horse-racing style. Vronsky divides all the bills he receives into three distinct categories, ranked in order of urgency of payment, and he never deviates from this system. He likewise has strict moral regulations for himself: he may lie to a woman but never to a man, and so on. On the whole, Tolstoy suggests that Vronsky is perhaps as much of a stickler for rational systems as the other Alexei, Anna's analytical husband. Karenin applies his methods to public policy, whereas Vronsky applies his to his finances. Regardless, it is clear that both men value intellectual systems over intuition, instinct, or whim. Tolstoy thus thwarts our expectation of a stark contrast between a cold, rational Karenin and a stormy, passionate Vronsky. The two are certainly different but not absolute opposites. Anna, who has little interest in applying systems of thought to her personal life, may be less similar to either of them than they are to each other. Indeed, she never once appeals to any rule or process of deduction to determine her actions. In her ruling instincts Anna resembles Levin more than her husband or her lover.

Vronsky's conversation with Anna at the country house is the first hint at a decline in the intimacy of their relations. For the first time in the novel we are aware of Vronsky having a thought that he fails to share with Anna—his memory of Serpukhovskoy's warning about the dangerous effects of women on men's ambition. Tolstoy heightens the drama of this moment at the country house by showing us Vronsky's thought and then telling us of his inability to communicate it to Anna. Serpukhovskoy's advice itself is not necessarily valid, for Anna has proved herself a capable wife to the extremely ambitious Karenin. What is more important is that the advice cannot be shared, which signals the formation of a boundary between Vronsky's mind and Anna's. As the novel progresses, this boundary becomes increasingly insurmountable and foreshadows the end of their union. Another hint of a bleak future comes in Vronsky's reference to Anna's "humiliation," a very public form of shame. Anna rightly rejects this term, saying she does not feel humiliation. She is aware only of love, a private emotion. Vronsky's focus on humiliation suggests that he feels beholden to the pressure of social values— a pressure that represents a clear danger to their love.

Just as Vronsky's rationality comes as a surprise, so do Levin's thoughts of mortality and of his own death. Though Levin is a healthy and vigorous man ablaze with future plans, Tolstoy has him meditate on death for several reasons. First, Levin's thoughts reveal his deep empathy with his critically ill brother. Like Anna, Levin is unable to distance himself from the suffering of anyone close to him. Second, Levin's reflections on mortality endow him with a wise humility that other characters, such as Karenin and even Vronsky, lack. Levin is no frailer than they, yet some vainglorious quality about those other men makes it hard to imagine either of them contemplating his own demise. Even Vronsky, who has come near death in the horse race, has not let the experience noticeably alter his views. Levin is different: his closeness to his ailing brother causes him to realize and accept his human nature and limited life span. Finally, Levin's thoughts of death align him with Anna, who thinks about death the first moment we meet her, after the casualty in the train station. Levin and Anna are linked not only in the intensity of their lives but also in their recognition of the closeness of death.

SUMMARY & ANALYSIS

PART FOUR, CHAPTERS I–XI

SUMMARY

The Karenins continue to live in the same house but are almost completely estranged from each other. Karenin makes it a rule to see Anna every day—in order to avoid spreading rumors of separation among the servants—but he never dines at home. Both husband and wife fervently hope that their painful situation is temporary.

Vronsky endures a dull week, entertaining a visiting foreign dignitary who wishes to experience the true spirit of Russia. Carousing with gypsy girls, the foreigner believes he is discovering Russian culture. Vronsky is pained by the resemblance between the foreigner and himself: both are healthy, confident, rather empty noblemen.

Returning home one night, Vronsky finds a note from Anna saying that she must see him, inviting him to her home when Karenin is to be at a meeting. Vronsky goes to Anna at the appointed time but is shocked to run into Karenin, whose meeting has ended early. Anna is grouchy, making barbed remarks about Vronsky's night with the foreigner and the gypsy girls. Vronsky is sadly aware of how Anna has changed, both morally and physically: she is irritable and has put on weight.

Anna erupts in anger toward Karenin, calling him a puppet and an "administrative machine" and reproaching his lack of guts. She says that in his place she would have killed a wife like herself. Vronsky attributes Anna's moodiness to her pregnancy, and asks when the baby is due. Anna says that it should not be long. She adds that soon everything will be resolved, as she will die shortly. Vronsky accuses Anna of speaking nonsense, but she declares that she has had a prophetic dream—a vision of an old peasant man rummaging in a sack and talking about the necessity of beating iron. The peasant in the dream told her that she would die in childbirth.

Karenin passes a sleepless night after his run-in with Vronsky, angered that Anna has violated the only condition he placed on her—that she never receive Vronsky in Karenin's house. Karenin tells Anna he plans to initiate divorce proceedings, and seizes her love letters from Vronsky to use as evidence. Anna begs Karenin to allow her to keep custody of Seryozha. Karenin replies that although he no longer loves the boy, he will take him anyway.

The next day, Karenin visits a divorce lawyer, who assumes Karenin wishes to pursue a mutually consenting divorce. Karenin explains that he wants to prove involuntary exposure of an adulterous affair, using the love letters as evidence. The lawyer warns him that such cases require the involvement of religious authorities, and that often letters are not sufficient evidence. The lawyer asks Karenin for freedom to proceed with the specifics of the divorce as he thinks best, and Karenin agrees.

After being thwarted by a rival at work, Karenin decides to set out for the provinces in an attempt to redeem his professional reputation. He encounters Stiva and Dolly one day and treats them coolly. Stiva, who is in good spirits and is enjoying his new ballerina mistress, invites Karenin, Levin, Kitty, and others to a dinner party. Karenin initially declines, revealing his plans to divorce Anna. Though Stiva is shocked and worried about his sister, he insists that Karenin come nonetheless. At the dinner party, Karenin is cold toward the others. Even so, the food is excellent and the party is successful. Kitty and Levin see each other for the first time since the failed marriage proposal, and their mutual love is overwhelmingly evident. Over dinner, the guests discuss education and the rights of women.

ANALYSIS

Anna's bizarre dream and her prophecy that her life will soon end deepen her association with death. Prior to this point in the novel, Anna has been linked to death only symbolically, through the death of the workman at the train station and through the black dress she wears when dancing with Vronsky. When Anna straightforwardly announces that she is convinced she will die in childbirth, the connection between her illicit love and her death is cemented. Her sense that death is approaching is not rational, as it is based solely on a dream—but Anna has never done anything for rational reasons, so her certainty about dying carries a great deal of weight. In one sense this dream is a simple device foreshadowing Anna's eventual death, accompanied by a note of the supernatural that suggests a divine force that punishes wrongdoers. But her death may be more than a tragic side effect of her love. Tolstoy hints that Anna may actually yearn for her own demise. When Anna rejects Karenin's restraint, saying that in his place she would have killed a wife like herself, her suicide fantasy is obvious. Death may come not as a punishment but as the only option for a desperate woman.

The specter of dishonesty pervades the Karenins' domestic life, as they still live together in purported harmony despite the reality of their near-complete estrangement. Karenin is so intent on maintaining the outward appearance of propriety that he makes a point of visiting Anna once a day merely so rumors will not spread among the servants. Anna's worst nightmare—prolonging her deceitful existence—is unfortunately now her way of life. She knows that this charade may continue indefinitely if Karenin refuses a divorce.

Tolstoy artfully broadens *Anna Karenina* into a social critique by showing how the Karenins' false lifestyle is not an anomaly but actually quite typical of other aristocratic Russians in the same social circle. Subtly, and without commentary or value judgment, the narrator mentions Stiva's new ballerina mistress, showing us that Stiva has not repented of his earlier offense to Dolly but has perhaps only learned to hide his misdemeanors more carefully. Similarly, Vronsky is aware that he is only mimicking typical Russian life with his foreign guest, playing at being the stereotypical high-living nobleman his guest expects to see. This universality of deceitful living among the Russian nobility makes their upcoming rejection of Anna all the more hypocritical.

Stiva's society dinner party seems a bit jarring, as it shows us that the carefree Stiva pursues his social calendar as usual even after receiving the shocking news that divorce proceedings are in the works against his sister. Though divorce may be commonplace in our society, in 1870s Russia it carried a great stigma, typically leaving the guilty party socially shunned, unable to remarry, and without custody of his or her children. In this light, we might expect a more sensitive brother to cancel his dinner party upon hearing such devastating news. Stiva, however, carries on with his soiree as scheduled. We cannot wholeheartedly blame Stiva, though, as he clearly loves his sister. Furthermore, we sense that he may be hoping to use the party to dissuade Karenin from divorce, though a private and solemn meeting at home would likely be more fitting than a festive dinner. Still, we have lingering doubts about the way Stiva and the other male characters in *Anna Karenina* treat women. As a novelist, Tolstoy was enormously sensitive to the situation of women in Russia. Here he implicitly criticizes the womanizing and oblivious Stiva: Anna may be ruined, but Stiva lets the party go on.

SUMMARY & ANALYSIS

PART FOUR, CHAPTERS XII–XXIII

SUMMARY

Over dinner at the Oblonskys', a guest makes a remark that displeases Karenin, who leaves the table. He finds Dolly in the drawing room and reveals to her his firm plans for divorce. Hearing that Anna has cheated on Karenin, Dolly protests that Anna will be ruined. Karenin claims there is nothing he can do.

At the same dinner, Levin and Kitty speak to each other for the first time since her rejection of his marriage proposal. Clearly still caring for each other greatly, they play a word game on a card table through which they apologize to each other for their past errors. Levin proposes to Kitty again, and she accepts. Later, Levin tells his brother Sergei of his engagement and wanders sleeplessly in the streets, overjoyed. When morning comes, Levin visits the Shcherbatsky house and embraces Kitty. In a happy daze, Levin goes off to buy flowers and presents for the engagement celebration. Levin, wishing to be fully honest with Kitty, shows her his journals, which divulge the fact that he is agnostic and has not been chaste prior to marriage. Kitty is upset but ultimately forgiving.

Karenin is passed over for a government post he has been coveting. Just after receiving this bad news, he receives a telegram announcing that Anna is gravely ill. He arrives to learn that Anna has delivered a baby girl, and that she is suffering from a fever from which she is not expected to recover. Vronsky is present at Anna's bedside. Anna is sure she is dying, so she begs Karenin for forgiveness. She also implores Karenin to forgive Vronsky, which Karenin tearfully does.

When Vronsky is about to leave the house, Karenin tells him that he has forgiven Anna and will stay by her side. Vronsky departs with the feeling that his love for Anna, which has flagged lately, is reviving. Back at his home, he cannot sleep, tormented by the possibility of Anna's death. Only half-aware of his actions, Vronsky aims a pistol at his chest and fires. He is gravely wounded but survives, as one of his servants quickly discovers him and sends for doctors.

Karenin, meanwhile, is surprised by how sincerely he was able to forgive Anna, and by the tenderness he feels toward her newborn daughter, who is also named Anna. Later, Karenin overhears a conversation between Anna and Betsy Tverskaya. Betsy implores Anna to say goodbye to Vronsky before he leaves for the provincial capital of Tashkent, where he is to be stationed. Anna refuses, saying that there is no point in seeing Vronsky again. On the way out, Betsy begs Karenin to allow Vronsky to visit Anna one last time. Karenin answers that such a matter is solely his wife's decision. In desperate grief, Anna privately affirms to Karenin that there is no point in seeing Vronsky again. Karenin says he is willing to allow the affair to continue, provided that the family and children are not disgraced.

Stiva arrives at the Karenin house. Anna privately tells him that she cannot stand Karenin any longer. Stiva says the problem is simple: Anna married someone whom she did not love and who was twenty years her senior; now she loves another man, and she must decide whether or not to stay with her husband. Anna says she does not know what to do. Stiva speaks to Karenin, who shows him a letter he has begun writing to Anna. The letter tells Anna that the decision about the future of their marriage is entirely in her hands. Stiva says that only divorce will satisfy Anna, but Karenin reminds him of the disgrace she will suffer if she chooses such a path. Stiva mentions that Karenin could allow Anna to escape public shame by taking responsibility for the disgrace himself—by pretending that it was he, rather than Anna, who committed adultery. Karenin tearfully says that he is willing to accept this option.

Vronsky, hearing that Karenin has granted a divorce, visits Anna. They acknowledge their mutual love. Anna says that Karenin is being too generous with her, so she cannot accept his magnanimity in granting her wish for divorce proceedings. Vronsky resigns his commission, and he and Anna set off on a trip abroad, abandoning the idea of divorce.

ANALYSIS

Levin's bliss at confirming his love for Kitty, and hearing her confirm it in return, is one of the most unforgettable portrayals of romantic love in all of literature. Yet this scene also fulfills a key function in the novel, reminding us of Tolstoy's interest in exploring the relationship between reason and instinct in human life. Levin's joy is irrational. His state approaches delirium as he loses control over his body and mind. He walks in the frigid Russian air without a coat, yet he does not feel cold. He tries to eat but feels no need of food, even though he has not eaten since the day before. He has not slept for two nights when he shows up in the morning at the Shcherbatsky residence in a blissful daze. This irrational episode puts Levin in stark contrast to Karenin, who, we suspect, has never had an irrational moment in his life. It also separates Levin from Vronsky, who always tries to maintain control over his life, as we see in his attempts to master Frou-Frou and settle his financial accounts methodically. Whereas Levin throws himself into love blindly and freely, Vronsky enters it in a controlling and self-possessed spirit. We ultimately sense that Tolstoy admires Levin's love far more.

Our view of Karenin is jolted in these chapters when he breaks into tears and volunteers to accept guilt in the divorce proceedings. The tears themselves are a shock, as we have been told that Karenin hates nothing more than crying, which he considers irrational and odious. Here, however, Karenin's intellectual and logical armor is pierced, and we get a glimpse of an emotional man within. Moreover, his assumption of guilt is unexpectedly and extraordinarily altruistic. As an important public personage, Karenin is well aware of the disgrace that would fall upon him and undoubtedly destroy his career. Honor is a paramount personal consideration for him—he says just a few chapters earlier that he is even willing to allow Anna to carry on her liaison as long as she does not threaten the honor of the family. Here, however, Karenin is willing not only to accept a divorce for Anna's sake but also to sacrifice his own honor in the bargain. This sudden selflessness utterly shakes up our view of Karenin's character, derailing our more cynical judgments about his attitude toward Anna's adultery. Karenin is no passionate hero, but he is not a machine, as Anna calls him, either.

Anna's deathbed plea for forgiveness for herself and Vronsky, and Karenin's surprising assent, raise important questions about the moral and theological importance of forgiveness in this novel. Several of the staple Christian teachings of selflessness—turning the other cheek to wrongdoers, giving away one's cloak when one's coat has been stolen, and so on—are repeatedly cited in *Anna Karenina*. Karenin, in his sudden generosity, exemplifies these tenets in his willingness to forgive and forget everything. We see similar generosity in Levin's and Kitty's forgiveness of each other's past decisions and actions. But forgiveness does not have a simple function in the novel; it is not a cure-all that can be universally offered and accepted. Indeed, the epigraph that begins *Anna Karenina* is a quotation from the New Testament (Romans 12:19) that evokes the harsher morality of the Old Testament from which it is borrowed (Deuteronomy 32:35): "Vengeance is mine; I shall repay." This emphasis on vengeance, the very opposite of forgiveness, suggests that violent retribution may ultimately win out over meek humility. Indeed, we see that Anna asks for Karenin's forgiveness but does not necessarily accept it, fleeing abroad with Vronsky at the end of Part Four. The role of forgiveness is not a clear-cut one in the world of the novel: though a powerful healing force in Levin and Kitty's relationship, it may ultimately be rejected in favor of vengeance in Karenin and Anna's.

PART FIVE, CHAPTERS I–XVI

SUMMARY

As Levin and Kitty's wedding date is set, Levin remains in his blissful daze. He performs all the duties expected of him but is almost mad with joy. Stiva reminds Levin that he must go to confession before his wedding. Levin meets with the priest and confesses that he doubts everything, including the existence of God. The priest sternly warns Levin that the Christianity of his future offspring is at stake. Later, Levin enjoys a bachelor party with his brother Sergei and Sergei's university friend, Katavasov. The bachelors ask Levin if he is prepared to give up his freedom for the constraints of marriage. Levin, feeling insecure and wondering why Kitty should ever love him at all, asks Kitty whether she wants to go through with the wedding. They have a brief argument but are reconciled.

That evening, the wedding guests await the groom in the church. Levin is late because a mix-up involving his clothes has left him without a proper shirt to wear. The ceremony is delayed and the guests become impatient, but Levin finally arrives at the church. Kitty cannot understand the priest's words as she hears them, for she is swept away by love. Levin cries during the ceremony. The wedding concludes majestically, and Levin and Kitty leave for his country estate.

Vronsky and Anna, meanwhile, travel in Italy for three months together and settle down and rent a palazzo. Vronsky, seeking distraction, is delighted to meet an old school friend, Golenishchev. Golenishchev and Anna get along well. Vronsky listens as Golenishchev expounds on the book he is writing, and Anna tells Golenishchev that Vronsky has taken up painting.

Anna, for her part, has been very happy. Far from Russia, she feels no more disgrace. Vronsky is less contented, however: all his desires are satisfied, so he misses desire itself. He begins to paint a portrait of Anna. Hearing of a Russian painter named Mikhailov who lives in their town, Vronsky reflects on the new generation of Russian intellectuals who have talent but lack education. Anna, intrigued, proposes visiting Mikhailov.

When Vronsky and Anna arrive at Mikhailov's studio, the artist is flattered to receive attention from wealthy Russians. He shows them a painting in progress, a scene from the life of Jesus Christ. Anna and Vronsky praise Mikhailov's rendering of Pontius Pilate, and Anna delights in the expression of pity on Jesus' face. The visitors enjoy even more a landscape painting of Russian boys relaxing by a river. Vronsky asks whether the latter painting is for sale and hires Mikhailov to paint Anna's portrait. Vronsky abandons his own portrait of Anna and becomes dissatisfied with their Italian life.

Levin slowly adjusts to married life. He imagines that Kitty needs only to be loved, forgetting that she has desires and aspirations of her own. Kitty throws herself into housekeeping with gusto in a way that initially annoys Levin but then pleases him. Quarrels occasionally erupt. One day, Levin gets lost on the way home from the fields, and Kitty is jealous and suspicious of where he has been. He is offended but then forgives her.

Meanwhile, Levin continues work on his book about the Russian agricultural system, but his slow progress distresses him. He chastises himself for being spoiled by married life, and silently reproaches Kitty for her lack of interest in anything other than housekeeping. Levin receives a letter from Marya Nikolaevna, saying that she is back with his brother Nikolai, who is dying of consumption. Levin says he must visit Nikolai, and Kitty insists on going with him. Levin does not want her to come, resenting his lack of freedom and shuddering at the idea of Kitty meeting a former prostitute. Levin and Kitty fight, but finally he allows her to come along.

SUMMARY & ANALYSIS

ANALYSIS

Levin's confession to the priest brings religion out from the background—where it has been consistently throughout *Anna Karenina*—and into focus in the foreground. Like many thinkers of his era, Tolstoy was skeptical of religious faith but also yearned for its potential for transcendence. In the novel, Tolstoy gives Levin—his namesake in the novel, as Lev is Tolstoy's first name—this same ambivalence toward religion. Levin is a deeply soulful person, as we see in his ecstasy in both farming and marriage. However, though he has the spirituality that faith demands, he lacks belief in its dogma and rituals. With characteristic candor, Levin tells the priest that he doubts the existence of God—a remarkable statement even for Levin. This contradiction, however, is exactly Tolstoy's point: Levin is in the church not because of faith but because of social convention, as a confession certificate is required for marriage. Tolstoy invites us to see religion as divided between spirituality on one hand and social expectations on the other. He does not attack religion but merely suggests that observance of its social institutions often replaces true spirituality.

Meanwhile, the account of Vronsky and Anna's time in Italy hints at the lovers' future difficulties as refugees from Russian social conventions. At first glance, they seem to live in an expatriate paradise: they are wealthy, have servants and a beautiful palazzo, and pass their time strolling and painting, with no enemies to attack or demean their love. Anna is happier than she ever imagined, and Vronsky feels that all his desires are satisfied. Nonetheless, there is trouble in this seeming paradise. Vronsky misses desire—in particular, we feel he misses the professional ambitions that guided his life in Russia. Even in exile, Russia draws the lovers back into its grip. Significantly, the people important to Anna and Vronsky in Italy are Russians—Golenishchev and Mikhailov. No Italians are significant enough to be named in the novel. The painting that Vronsky loves most is not the portrait of Jesus—a rebel like him and Anna—but rather a Russian landscape. For all his love of Italy, Vronsky is pulled back toward the very country where he and his lover are damned, defiled, and excluded. Social conventions, we see, are not easy to escape. They are part of us, and we continue to live within them even when suffering because of them.

As Tolstoy continues to develop the plots involving Levin and Anna in parallel, he invites us to compare the differing honeymoons of the novel's two recently formalized romantic relationships. Despite the fact that Levin's majestic church wedding contrasts starkly with Anna's scandalous flight to Italy, the two unions are surprisingly similar. The difference between their respective legal statuses hardly matters when we focus on their internal dynamics. Both couples settle in the countryside, leaving behind social ambitions, and both struggle with the disorientation that comes from having their desires satisfied. Vronsky finds total satisfaction to be irksome, and Levin admits to Kitty that he is discontented even though he is happy. Both men are unable to do the work they dream of doing: Vronsky is antsy after resigning from his regiment, and Levin cannot bring himself to work on his book on agriculture. The similarities between Vronky and Levin remind us not to exaggerate the importance of Anna's so-called immorality. Relationships are relationships whether or not they bear social or religious stamps of approval. Tolstoy encourages us to look beyond social rules and to examine the inner workings of romantic unions with an open mind.

PART FIVE, CHAPTERS XVII–XXXIII

SUMMARY

In a dingy hotel in the provinces, Levin meets Nikolai, who is clearly at death's door. Kitty insists on seeing Nikolai too, and he greets her pleasantly. Levin cannot bear to look at Nikolai, but the more practical Kitty immediately gets down to work to lessen the dying man's suffering, displaying remarkable compassion and empathy for him. Kitty's tenderness touches Nikolai. Levin meditates on how he fears death more than Kitty, even though he is more intelligent than she. He concludes that he is self-centered whereas she is selfless.

The next day, Nikolai takes communion and feels better, passing a half-hour without coughing. But then the cough returns. Nikolai tells Kitty—whom he calls by her Russian name, Katia—to leave the room, as he will die soon. He continues to linger between life and death, however. Kitty, meanwhile, feels ill and vomits. After several tedious days of waiting, Nikolai finally passes away. The doctor tells Kitty that she is vomiting because she is pregnant.

Karenin, meanwhile, cannot grasp what has led him to his current misery. Asked to pay one of Anna's overdue bills, he nearly breaks down. His career is at a standstill. The narrator fills us in on Karenin's childhood: an orphan, Karenin grew up with many awards and distinctions but without intimacy in his life. Now, his friend Lydia Ivanovna urges him to trust in Jesus and offers to run his household. Forlornly in love with Karenin herself, Lydia Ivanovna has replaced erotic passion with religious love. However, she is spiteful toward Anna, refusing to acknowledge Anna's letter pleading to see Seryozha. Lydia Ivanovna informs Karenin that Anna is in St. Petersburg, which makes Karenin glum. He asserts that he cannot thwart Anna's maternal love for her son. Lydia Ivanovna maliciously asks whether Anna truly loves her son.

Seryozha's birthday arrives, and his joy in getting gifts is heightened by his pride that his father has received an official award. The boy bombards his tutor with questions about his father's award, but the tutor insists he concentrate on schoolwork. Seryozha wonders why the tutor does not love him. Lydia Ivanovna has told Seryozha that his mother is dead to him, but he still hopes to see Anna again. Karenin visits Seryozha and quizzes him on his religious lessons. Seryozha does not do well, and Karenin is disappointed in his son's progress.

Upon returning to St. Petersburg, Vronsky and Anna stay in a fine hotel. They hope to resume their social life but are thwarted. Everyone shuns them, even Betsy Tverskaya, who explains that she cannot risk the public shame of socializing with Anna. Anna receives Karenin's denial of her plea to see Seryozha and is devastated. Determined to see her son anyway, she buys him toys for his birthday and visits the Karenin home one morning, hiding her face until she has entered.

The servants recognize Anna and bring her to Seryozha. Mother and son chat, and Anna cries with joy and regret. Seryozha's former nanny, also visiting him, informs Anna that Karenin is soon to enter the room. Anna hurries away but encounters Karenin on her way out. As she leaves, she realizes that she never got the chance to give Seryozha his toys. Returning to the hotel in a daze, Anna is unable to fathom her present situation. Moreover, she suddenly feels less love toward her infant daughter, Annie. Anna mentally reproaches Vronsky for abandoning her lately.

Vronsky returns to the hotel to find Anna with Princess Oblonskaya, an old, unmarried aunt of Anna's with a bad reputation. Anna announces that she plans to attend the opera that evening. Vronsky begs her not to, warning her of the fact that the members of high society at the theater will scorn and humiliate her. He believes that she wishes to deliberately provoke and insult conventional society.

Nevertheless, Anna leaves for the opera. Vronsky follows later and watches in horror as Anna is insulted by acquaintances in the neighboring box. Anna returns home angry and desperate. Vronsky reassures her of his love, and the two depart for the countryside.

ANALYSIS

Just before we see Anna reach the depths of humiliation in her public disgrace, Tolstoy shows us a glimpse of Anna in private, at her most tender and maternal moment. The author juxtaposes the two extremes of Anna's personality: just as we have never seen her so brazenly in the public eye as during her time at the opera, so too have we never seen her quite so loving and motherly as when she secretly brings birthday presents to her son. We have frequently heard that she loves Seryozha, but her tears of joy at seeing him prove that love. The birthday scene is crucial because it reminds us that the love for which Anna lives is not just romantic love but parental love as well. Her life is defined by the fact that she cares for certain people and does not care for others. In this regard, she is not a dizzy romantic dreamer like Flaubert's deluded Madame Bovary. Anna does not throw away her past in pursuit of a dashing love interest but simply and passionately tries to find and stick by true love in all its forms, whether lover or son.

These chapters all center on human isolation, exploring this concept from different angles through the experiences of different characters. Karenin's loneliness nearly pushes him to a nervous breakdown as his family life and professional career fall apart. The man who once seemed invincible now appears surprisingly frail. Tolstoy suggests that isolation can topple even giants. We learn that Karenin was an orphan, raised without parental intimacy. In giving us Karenin's childhood history, the author invites us to conclude that Karenin's later pursuit of status and honor is an attempt to fill the void left by the lack of family love. Seryozha may well feel this same lack of love, and we fear that he may grow up to be just like his father. When Seryozha asks his tutor about official awards and wonders why the tutor does not love him more, we see that the boy mixes intimacy and honors in his mind as much as his father does.

Anna's humiliation in the theater is, of course, another case of isolation—a painful, forced ostracism. The dying Nikolai is isolated as well, and Kitty's companionship is like a medicine to him. Though Nikolai does not recover, Kitty's kindness makes his final days far less lonely and frightening than they might have been. The healing power of Kitty's company for Nikolai reminds us that simple togetherness can have a miraculous effect in curing the great ill of isolation that afflicts mankind.

PART SIX, CHAPTERS I–XVI

SUMMARY

Dolly, unhappy with her own run-down estate, moves in with Levin and Kitty for the summer. Kitty's friend Varenka and Levin's half-brother, Sergei, are also present. Sergei is friendly despite the others' awe of his fame. Dolly and Kitty even discuss the possibility of setting him up with Varenka. Levin is skeptical of this idea, explaining that Sergei is used to a spiritual life whereas Varenka is more earthy. Levin tells Kitty that he envies Sergei, who lives for duty and thus can reach satisfaction. Kitty asks why Levin is not satisfied himself. Levin mentions his work frustrations but affirms he is happy overall.

Sergei and Varenka do indeed like each other greatly, and Sergei fantasizes about proposing marriage. One day, the two go out picking mushrooms together, and both of them suddenly realize Sergei is on the verge of proposing. At the last minute, however, he is unable to bring himself to do so, as he wishes to be loyal to the memory of a deceased lover from his youth. The opportunity gone, Sergei and Varenka both realize they will never marry each other.

One day, Stiva arrives with a friend, the handsome Veslovsky. Stiva mentions that Veslovsky has visited Anna. Dolly asserts that she will visit Anna too, though Kitty is reluctant to go. Veslovsky flirts with Kitty, which makes Levin insanely jealous. Levin and Kitty quarrel and Levin apologizes, promising to make Veslovsky feel welcome on their hunting trip the next day.

Setting out with Stiva and Veslovsky, Levin is ashamed of his earlier anger, for he now finds Veslovsky comical and good-natured. But once they begin hunting, the presence of the somewhat hapless Veslovsky again bothers Levin, distracting him and causing him to shoot badly. The others bag far more game, and Levin's irritation grows. Veslovsky stupidly sets his gun off accidentally and gets their cart stuck in a marsh.

The men discuss a railroad magnate neighbor whose fortune Levin disdains, considering it ill gotten, the product of financial tricks, not hard work. Stiva mocks Levin for being a nobleman who does not work for his fortune, and Levin is irked. Levin goes to bed frustrated, while the other two go off in pursuit of farm girls, which Stiva says is acceptable as long as his wife does not find out.

Waking early the next morning, Levin goes off hunting alone. His dog flushes out several enormous snipe, which Levin kills effortlessly. Delighted, Levin returns hours later with nineteen birds. His joy disperses, however, when he learns that Stiva and Veslovsky have eaten all the food. Kitty then discusses her need to go to Moscow to see an obstetrician. Levin initially resists, believing doctors to be unnecessary, but finally assents. Veslovsky engages Kitty in a conversation about whether love can be above social conventions, but she finds his tone objectionable. Kitty and Levin quarrel and make up once more. Finally, Levin, again annoyed at Veslovsky's flirtation with Kitty, kicks him out of the house, despite his awareness that such an action is ungracious.

Dolly sticks to her plan of visiting Anna. She plans to hire her own horses rather than ask for Levin's, as she is reluctant to seek his aid for a potentially shameful mission. Levin, however, insists on giving Dolly his horses. During the trip, Dolly reflects on love and marriage, remembering a peasant girl's comment that motherhood is bondage. She understands Anna's need to live her life on her own terms, and wonders whether she too could love and be loved in a real way.

ANALYSIS

It might seem puzzling that Tolstoy suddenly chooses to focus on the courtship of two fairly marginal characters, Sergei and Varenka, at a point in the novel when Levin's and Anna's relationships are in full swing. However, the endearing and awkward romance between these two minor characters offers us an important contrast to other instances of love we glimpse in the novel, and makes us reflect on the nature of relationships in general. Sergei and Varenka are both spiritual creatures: Sergei is a born intellectual, and Varenka is often termed a born saint. They both seem to dwell in the air rather than in the flesh. Levin and Kitty are both aware of their differences from these two: Levin cannot follow Sergei's highly analytical approach to life's questions, and Kitty cannot follow Varenka's example of moral good works at the German spa. But Tolstoy suggests that spiritual gifts may be a disadvantage in life and love, as we watch Sergei and Varenka's touching but pathetic attempt to make romantic contact. Sergei dreams of declaring his love but ultimately can only dare talk about mushrooms. Their limitations are clear. Tolstoy may value purity of mind and heart, but he appreciates the worldly wisdom of physical beings still more.

Levin's hunting frustrations give us an interesting insight into his psyche. His difficulty in bagging game may be attributed to simple bad luck, or to the annoyance of having others nearby—but it may also go much deeper. When Tolstoy shows Levin's annoyance with Veslovsky, we suspect that the reason for Levin's poor shooting may be unconscious anger. He certainly resents Veslovsky's flirtations with Kitty, as we have seen earlier. Levin's irritation, however, may also have a philosophical and social dimension: he may be angry at the irresponsible lifestyles these Russian noblemen enjoy. Veslovsky—whose name contains the Russian word for "merrily," *veselo*—lives for pleasure and thinks only of himself. He nearly shoots his comrades by accident and laughs about it later, and he gets the cart stuck in the marsh through pure obliviousness. Veslovsky and Stiva also gobble up the food meant for Levin, again simply without thinking. On the whole, Veslovsky's womanizing and pleasure seeking are exaggerations of similar traits in Stiva, and they symbolize the harmful selfishness of the Russian noble classes that Levin generally dislikes. Levin wishes to care for and be mindful of something larger than his own urges; these other men do not.

Dolly's decision to visit Anna is an extraordinarily significant event. It reveals not just Dolly's strength of character—she dares to call on a woman shunned by society, simply because she loves her—but also a dimension of Dolly's inner thoughts that we have not seen before. Her willingness to hire her own horses, rather than use Levin's for fear of shaming him, shows that she is well aware of the stigma that her visit may bring. We never doubt Dolly's true love for Anna in paying her this visit, as Dolly is nothing if not sincere in her expression of affection. But on a deeper level, Dolly mentally puts herself in Anna's place throughout her trip, vicariously trying out Anna's experiences. Although happily devoted to her children, Dolly wistfully recalls overhearing a peasant say that motherhood is bondage. Dolly goes on to associate Anna with a freedom from this bondage, for Anna has abandoned her son. Anna represents freedom and happiness for Dolly, and her example is provocative, prompting Dolly to think about her own life philosophically. The climax of Dolly's interior monologue comes when she wonders whether she could be loved in a real way—hinting that she knows that the slick Stiva does not have real love for her.

PART SIX, CHAPTERS XVII–XXXII

SUMMARY

En route to Anna's house, Dolly encounters Anna, Veslovsky, Princess Oblonskaya, and Levin's friend Sviyazhsky on horseback. Dolly is startled by Anna's boldness in riding horseback, which society considers improper for ladies. Dolly dislikes Princess Oblonskaya, who sponges off of her rich relatives. Dolly knows that she looks older than Anna. Anna speaks of her great, "unforgivable" happiness: having survived past fears and torments, she says she only wants to live. She talks about Vronsky's estate management and the first-class hospital he is building for the local peasant community.

Dolly stays in a room that Anna calls inferior but that is in fact very luxurious. Dolly feels very self-conscious about her shabby clothes. Anna presents her baby daughter, who is illegitimate but technically a Karenin. Dolly is troubled by the child's disagreeable governess and by Anna's ignorance of nursery matters. Indeed, Anna even admits she feels superfluous in the infant's upbringing. Overall, Anna's life pleases Dolly, who envies Anna's freedom and love. In private, Vronsky implores Dolly to persuade Anna to get a divorce—which Karenin had agreed to earlier—so that Vronsky and Anna might petition the emperor for a legal adoption of their daughter. Dolly promises to speak to Anna later.

Over a costly dinner, the group discusses such topics as American efficiency in building, government abuses, and the *zemstvo* system. When someone mentions that Levin has retired from *zemstvo* activity, Vronsky asserts that it is important for a nobleman to fulfill his duties, as he does in serving as justice of the peace. Dolly, annoyed by Vronsky's slighting of Levin, affirms Levin's responsible character. Anna remarks that Vronsky's official duties are distancing him from her.

Playing croquet afterward, Dolly dislikes Veslovsky's flirtations with Anna. Later, Anna inquires about Levin, wanting the best for Kitty. Dolly mentions Anna's possible divorce for the sake of future children. Anna announces that because of her illness she can have no more children, saying she thinks it is for the best. Dolly wonders how Anna will hold on to Vronsky when her beauty inevitably fades. Anna says she cannot humiliate herself by writing to Karenin for a divorce. Dolly suddenly reflects on her own family life with warmth, noting that Anna takes medicine to fall asleep. Rather than stay several days as planned, Dolly decides to return home the next day.

When Vronsky announces he must travel to Kashin province for some important local elections, Anna receives the news with a strange calm. Levin, now living in Moscow because of Kitty's pregnancy, also goes to the elections. He is frustrated by the bureaucratic proceedings, but Sergei explains to him the importance of the elections, in which the old-guard marshal of nobility will be replaced by a younger man more supportive of the *zemstvo* system. When the vote is cast, the younger party wins. Levin runs into the landowner he met during his visit to Sviyazhsky's house and has a conversation with him. The landowner says that the elections have little significance and reports that he is still farming at a net loss; in fact, he is pessimistic about the state of Russian landowners in general. Levin tells Sviyazhsky, who is also present at the elections, that the local court is an idiotic institution.

Soon, Levin grows dejected and yearns to flee the elections. Ultimately, a venomous nobleman named Nevedovsky is elected marshal of the nobility. Vronsky hosts a party for the victor but receives a worried note from Anna telling him to return home immediately, as their infant daughter is ill. At home, Anna fumes over her utter lack of freedom, her inability to travel on a whim as Vronsky can. Vronsky returns and asks why Anna is irritable, once again affirming his love for her. Anna says she refuses to be separated from Vronsky again. She agrees to write Karenin for a divorce, which they expect him to permit.

ANALYSIS

In this section, Tolstoy uses the dinner party discussion of local politics to explore the notion of social commitment. Vronsky comes across as high-minded in his eloquent assertion that Russian nobles must serve their governmental duties, affirming a vital political and social role for the aristocracy. But his praise of social duty may be hollow, an idea put forth for show but lacking substance—just like Vronsky's state-of-the-art hospital, which seems to have been constructed more with the aim of being an architectural wonder than a practical facility. Vronsky may feel lofty social sentiments, but we trust Levin more, understanding his complaints that the local courts are bureaucratic and inefficient. Levin has had more hands-on political experience than Vronsky, having served on a *zemstvo,* so we give his cynicism about Russian local politics more weight. Moreover, the local elections at Kashin make us feel the futility of local social institutions even more sharply. Despite all the fanfare, most local landowners appear to agree that the vote is meaningless. All the bluster and attention leads to nothing of importance. As Vronsky figures large in the elections, we may associate this empty bluster with his character.

Tolstoy's brand of feminism, in the sense of attention to the political and social oppression of the women of his era, is strongly evident in these chapters, beginning with the unforgettable portrait of Dolly meeting the happy Anna on horseback. At the time, as the narrator hints, it was almost scandalous for a grown woman to ride on horseback. Tolstoy thus purposely portrays Anna in a radically unconventional pose. The symbolic contrast with Dolly is noticeable. We note that Dolly's journey to Anna's house is enabled entirely by men: Dolly is transported by a male driver, on horses borrowed from another man, Levin. Anna, on the other hand, is in control of her own movement, guiding the horse directly. When Dolly compares herself to Anna immediately upon meeting her, noting the differences in the aging of their faces, we feel that Dolly is already envious of Anna's independence and its benefits. Yet Tolstoy reminds us that Anna's independence is far from complete, noting how she fumes over the fact that Vronsky enjoys far greater rights than she. Vronsky can travel at will, while she is stuck at home. Symbolically, Anna is on the road to women's emancipation but has not yet arrived.

Tolstoy's treatment of motherhood here may indicate the limitations of his feminist sympathies. As Anna pursues her freedom, Tolstoy deprives her of a maternal role—not only does she lose custody of Seryozha and feel ambivalence toward her baby girl, but her illness also leaves her unable to have any more children. Some readers feel that Tolstoy demonstrates an old-fashioned sexism in insisting that an independent woman automatically becomes both infertile and a bad mother. But we should not necessarily label Tolstoy a misogynist. The sexist ideas that appear here—such as Dolly's idea that Anna will be unable to keep Vronsky after her beauty fades, which equates a woman's desirability only with her physical appearance—are not necessarily Tolstoy's. The author may circulate ideas that provoke dissent and reflection in the reader without agreeing with them himself. In any case, we must exercise caution in assessing Tolstoy's views toward women.

PART SEVEN, CHAPTERS I–XVI

SUMMARY

In Moscow, Levin and Kitty await the birth of their child. Kitty notes how anxious and wary Levin is in the city compared to the countryside. He dislikes the men's club and its attendant socializing but has few other ways to pass the time. In her condition, Kitty rarely goes out. On one occasion, however, she does leave the house and encounters Vronsky, whom she addresses calmly, pleased at her ability to master her former romantic feelings for him.

Levin is uncomfortably aware of the expenses of city life, noting that the cost of his city servants' uniforms could pay for two summer workers on his farm. He meets the scholars Katavasov and Metrov and discusses his book on Russian agriculture with them. Metrov is agreeable but understands agricultural issues solely in terms of capital and wages, ignoring the cultural factors that are central to Levin's thinking. Levin concludes that intellectual advancement can come only from each scholar following his own ideas to the end. He leaves to visit Lvov, the diplomat husband of Kitty's sister Natalie. Lvov complains about the studying required to keep up with his children's education, which he supervises.

Levin then goes to a concert and hears an orchestral piece based on Shakespeare's *King Lear*. Levin dislikes the piece's random connection of disparate moods, and the audience's enthusiastic applause perplexes him. Later, at a reception, Levin discusses a recently concluded trial and finds himself repeating words that he heard someone else say the day before. Then Levin goes to the club, where he enjoys lewd and drunken conversation with Stiva, Vronsky, and others, laughing so loudly that others turn to look. Levin decides he likes Vronsky. Stiva asks Levin whether he likes the gentlemen's club—their "temple of idleness"—and notes how lazy some of the members are. Levin gambles and loses forty rubles. Stiva suddenly proposes a surprise visit to Anna, whom Levin has never met. Levin agrees. Stiva explains Anna's loneliness in Moscow, saying that she passes her time writing a children's book and assisting in the education of the daughter of an impoverished English family.

Stiva and Levin reach Anna's home, where Levin immediately notices Mikhailov's portrait of her. Anna delights Levin with her sincerity, beauty, and intelligence. The two discuss a variety of topics in an easy and familiar way, and Levin is amazed by Anna's grace and facility in conversation. Levin asks why Anna supports the English girl but not Russian schoolchildren. Anna replies that she only loves this particular girl, and love is paramount. On parting, Anna tells Levin that she does not wish Kitty to forgive her, for forgiveness would be possible only if Kitty were to live through the same nightmare Anna has experienced. Levin blushes and agrees to tell Kitty.

Levin returns home, aware of his fascination with and attraction to Anna. He tells Kitty he has met Anna, and Kitty jealously provokes a quarrel. Meanwhile, Anna, alone, wonders why Vronsky is colder to her than Levin. When Vronsky returns, she chastises him for preferring his male friends to her. Vronsky notes the clear hostility in her tone. Anna speaks vaguely and ominously about a disaster she is nearing and about her fear of herself.

Surprising even himself, Levin grows accustomed to his expensive and superficial city life. One night, Kitty awakens him with news that her labor has begun. Levin is dazed, aware only of her suffering and the need to alleviate it. He picks up the doctor, frustrated by delays. During the long labor, Levin becomes convinced that Kitty will die during childbirth. When the doctor announces that the birth has taken place, Levin can hardly believe he has a son. Kitty is fine, but the sight of the red, shrieking infant makes Levin feel a bizarre mix of pity and revulsion.

ANALYSIS

The meeting between Anna and Levin is a key structural point in the novel, as the parallel story lines converge and the two most emotionally intense characters in the work finally come face to face. Lost in the immensity of Tolstoy's novel, we may not even initially realize that this is the first time the two protagonists meet. Postponed for so long, the encounter acquires symbolic importance. The result is harmonious, as Levin and Anna like each other and connect easily. Indeed, it is hard to avoid speculating on what a marriage between Anna and Levin might have been like. Beyond a physical attraction, they seem to share a social and spiritual connection. The frequently awkward Levin has no difficulty conversing with Anna, and he never finds her artificial, as he finds many others. Levin's awareness that in Anna there is "truth," as he calls it, highlights the dogged search for sincerity that both these protagonists have led throughout the novel. Levin knows he is besotted with Anna, as his reflections on the way home make clear. Moreover, Kitty's jealousy of

Anna hints that she feels Levin's infatuation too. Of course, nothing comes of this interaction between Anna and Levin. The meeting simply invites us to compare their characters directly and to note the affinities between their respective searches for truth.

These chapters also give us a glimpse into Anna's increasingly strange and unstable mindset as she begins to slip into suicidal feelings. She is clearly tormented, yet it is striking how little objective cause for torment there is. To be sure, Anna's social life is no bed of roses, but earlier we see her radiantly happy in her outsider status when Dolly meets her on horseback. Anna blames Vronsky for coldness toward her, yet Vronsky's readiness to adapt to her plans and his promptness in answering her telegrams hardly appear coldhearted. She reproaches Vronsky for spending time with his male friends, but his socializing does not appear excessive. It would surely be unreasonable for her to expect Vronsky to spend every waking moment with her. Indeed, Anna admits in her apologetic note that her accusations are unfair. Yet we should not judge Anna too harshly; for it seems cruel to accuse her of making it all up, hysterically inventing reasons to be anguished. Her need for love at this time in her life—having abandoned son, husband, friends, and society—is overwhelming. As she repeatedly tells Vronsky, love is all she has left. We may feel that nothing is objectively wrong in Anna's life, but for her, subjective feelings of love are more important than objective physical well-being.

King Lear on the Heath, the fictional musical fantasia that Levin hears performed, is based on Shakespeare's great tragedy about isolation and mistrusted love, in which the hero, Lear, spends an anguished night on the moors confronting his own madness. Lear ends up alienated from others—an alienation that we see mirrored in both Levin's and Anna's experiences. Both Levin and Anna seek peace of mind in the country, yet both are disappointed when they withdraw into solitude only to discover their private demons—Levin's dissatisfaction with his unproductive life and Anna's furiously jealous fits. Moreover, Lear's rejection of the love of his affectionate daughter Cordelia reminds us of Anna's forthcoming rejection of Vronsky's love. In both Anna's and Lear's stories, a powerful emotion is the turning point of the plot. The reference to *King Lear* reminds us of the intensely subjective focus of *Anna Karenina.* The status of Tolstoy's novel as a realist work full of historical references sometimes threatens to obscure the fact that it is centrally about the human heart. While social themes are clearly present, *Anna Karenina* is anchored in the psychological states of its main protagonists, and the way they perceive reality colors the entire sweep of the novel.

PART SEVEN, CHAPTERS XVII–XXXI

SUMMARY

> "*Respect was invented to cover the empty place where love should be. But if you don't love me, it would be better and more honest to say so.*"
>
> (See QUOTATIONS, p. 77)

The Oblonskys' finances worsen, and Dolly demands control over her portion of their fortune. The family does not have enough money to pay the bills. Stiva resolves to get a cushy appointment on a railroad commission. He goes to St. Petersburg to speaks to Karenin about the job, as well as about his sister, Anna. Karenin claims that Anna's life no longer interests him but promises to give Stiva a definitive answer about the divorce the next day. On his way out, Stiva meets Seryozha, who is now an older schoolboy who claims not to remember his mother. Stiva then visits Betsy Tverskaya and talks to the freethinking Princess Miagky. The latter calls Karenin stupid, saying he has become a follower of a famous French psychic named Landau.

Stiva visits Lydia Ivanovna and meets Karenin and Landau. Stiva tries to talk about Anna, but Lydia will talk only of religion. They discuss theology at length. Lydia believes that man is saved by faith alone—not, as Stiva believes, through good deeds. When Lydia reads aloud from a religious tract, Stiva and Landau fall into a slumber. Stiva awakens to hear Landau—who is allegedly talking in his sleep—tell an unidentified woman to leave the room. The next day, Karenin informs Stiva that he has decided, based on Landau's dream speech, to refuse Anna's request for a divorce.

Anna and Vronsky continue to reside in Moscow, though their relationship is tense and unhappy. Anna is deeply jealous and paranoid, feeling that Vronsky no longer loves her and making unfounded assertions that he must be involved with another woman. Anna knows she is being unfair but cannot control her emotions. She and Vronsky argue about women's rights and women's education, which he dismisses. Vronsky tries to hide Stiva's telegram informing him that Karenin will not grant a divorce, but Anna demands to know Karenin's decision and says she accepts it.

Anna decides that she and Vronsky must go to the country immediately. Vronsky agrees to go but says he must finish some business with his mother first. Anna demands that he go now or not at all, and she even slights Vronsky's mother. Vronsky asks Anna to respect his mother, but Anna criticizes the whole idea of respect, calling it a replacement for love. Anna becomes more miserable, and Vronsky's attempts to appease her fail. For the first time ever, they quarrel for an entire day. Anna is convinced their relationship is over, and she falls into despair. Vronsky departs to visit his mother.

After Vronsky leaves for the train station, Anna regrets her unfair treatment of him and sends an apologetic note asking to speak to him. She reflects that she wants only to live and that she knows they love each other deeply. Later, Anna sends Vronsky a telegram requesting he return immediately.

Restless, and not having received a response, Anna drives to Dolly's to say farewell. Kitty hesitates to greet Anna but finally emerges and feels sympathy for her. Anna drives home, reflecting on the fact that all humans hate one another. She receives a curt telegram from Vronsky saying he cannot return before ten o'clock. Anna grows furious, interpreting the reply as a cold dismissal. She resolves to go meet Vronsky at the station.

> "No, you're going in vain. . . . You won't get away from yourselves."
>
> (See QUOTATIONS, p. 78)

On the way, Anna reflects on the Moscow cityscape and on the fact that Vronsky's love has faded. She thinks he feels only duty—not love—toward her. At the station, Anna feels disoriented, focusing on the fakeness of the people in the crowd and hardly knowing why she is there or what destination to request. She boards the train and despises the artificiality of her fellow passengers.

Stepping off the train as it stops at Obiralovka, Anna walks along the platform in a despairing daze, finally resolving to throw herself under an approaching train in order to punish Vronsky and be "rid of everybody and of herself." A train approaches, and Anna impulsively throws herself under the wheels, begging God for forgiveness and feeling a pang of confusion and regret when it is too late. The candle of her life is extinguished.

ANALYSIS

The surprising revelation that Karenin—seemingly the most rational of people—is under the sway of a French psychic forces us to reassess his character. His slide from a responsible and powerful government minister to a lonely and confused man with a stalled career proceeds with startling rapidity. We see the extent of Karenin's fall in the ridiculous scene in which he goes to sleep under Landau's influence. The very man who epitomizes rationalism and normalcy early in the novel is now guided by the flighty comments of a man who is likely a complete scam. Tolstoy highlights the French nationality of the psychic and has him deliver his odd prophecies in French (even within the original Russian text)—gestures that poke fun at the French cultural tradition, which prides itself on being rational. Tolstoy suggests that an excessive cult of reason in any culture may be just as misguided as the most outrageous occultism. Both extremes are opposed to the grounded experience of life from which Levin learns. Levin devotes himself simply to his wish to live life, rather than to visionary or mathematical theories of existence. Consequently, Tolstoy implies, Levin succeeds where others produce empty phrases and—like Karenin in the end—lead empty lives.

Tolstoy's brilliance as a literary psychologist is evident in the last and biggest of the quarrels that plague Anna and Vronsky's relationship. In literal terms, Anna's anger makes no sense. Vronsky has shown himself to be agreeably flexible in assenting to Anna's travel plans, only requesting that they leave a bit later so he can finish some transactions for his mother. Anna explodes in response to this seemingly reasonable request. Her outburst is not logical but suggests something deeper happening in her psyche. Anna's fury at Vronsky's mother and her resentment at his request that she "respect" Countess Vronsky stem from Anna's criticism of the very notion of respect. She makes this criticism explicit when she says that respect is a poor substitute for love. It is likely that Anna briefly identifies with the Countess as a recipient of Vronsky's dutiful respect rather than his passionate love. What Anna fears more than anything is what she abhorred in Karenin—that Vronsky feels duty toward her but nothing more.

Anna's death scene is justifiably considered one of the greatest of Tolstoy's achievements in the novel, and in Russian literature as a whole. Her suicide is not merely the end of her life but also its summation: she acts independently and alone, and she seeks to escape the falsity of the people around her, just as she did in life. Yet Anna is not a diva in death, any more than she was in life. She does not pity herself or appeal to the sympathy of the crowd; she does not care about what other people think of her. Anna does not fancy herself superior to anyone but rather includes herself in the group of people that she wishes to get rid of—she escapes not just the world but Anna Karenina as well. Tolstoy's portrayal of Anna's final minutes is filled not with the wrath and vengeance that the novel's epigraph foretells but rather with great tenderness. His description of Anna's life as a candle being illuminated and then snuffed out forever equates her life with light and truth. Tolstoy pays a quiet tribute to this character of whom he disapproves but whom he loves nonetheless.

PART EIGHT

SUMMARY

> "... [M]y life now ... is not only not meaningless, as it was before, but has the unquestionable meaning of the good which it is in my power to put into it!"
>
> (See QUOTATIONS, p. 79)

Two months pass after Anna's death. Sergei Koznyshev's book on statehood in Russia and Europe, on which he spent six years of work, is published to virtually no public recognition. Sergei tries to forget his failure by focusing his attention on the movement to liberate the Serbs, Montenegrins, and other Slavic groups from the Muslim rule of Turkey—a cause that seemingly occupies the whole Russian nation.

Sergei and Katavasov accompany a large number of Russian volunteers who are traveling to occupied Serbia to offer military support to the Slavs. A bystander affirms that Vronsky is among the volunteers, and that he has even outfitted a squadron at his own expense. Stiva appears from the crowd and greets Sergei. "God Save the Tsar" resounds from the patriotic crowd. Sergei meets Vronsky's mother, who is accompanying her son. The Countess Vronsky insults the dead Anna as "mean and low" and says that Karenin has taken custody of Anna's young daughter. Finally, Sergei speaks to Vronsky, who is ready and willing to die for the Slavic cause, as nothing in life has value for him now.

Sergei and Katavasov visit Levin's estate. Kitty greets them and feeds her infant son, Mitya, while waiting for Levin to come home.

She is glad Levin has visitors, for she has been worrying about his gloomy mood, which she attributes to his lack of religious faith. Levin has been more focused on philosophical questions ever since marriage and fatherhood, searching for the meaning of life. He has read the classics of philosophical idealism, seeking a non-materialist answer to his question. Unable to find any, he has flirted with suicide. When Levin stops thinking and simply lives, he finds himself happy.

The day Sergei arrives, Levin is tormented by seeing his peasant workers and imagining them dead and forgotten in a few years. Levin speaks to a peasant, Fyodor, about a local innkeeper who rents some nearby farmland. Fyodor explains that the innkeeper lives only for his belly, unlike many who live for God and goodness.

Fyodor's words galvanize Levin. He recognizes that living for God and goodness is the answer to his questions about the meaning of life. He feels freed from life's deceptions. Living for oneself and aiming only to satisfy one's own desires is childish, as Levin notes when he catches his children behaving mischievously. Life is good, whereas thinking is bad. The sky is not infinite but a vault overhead, however irrational that may be.

Lying on his back in a field, gazing up at the sky, Levin knows he has found faith and thanks God for it. He resolves never to allow quarrels or estrangement to divide him from other people. Just a few minutes later, however, Levin argues with his driver on the way back home after meeting Sergei and Katavasov. Levin feels self-critical but knows that his faith will survive despite his little moral failures. At home, he meets Dolly and her children, tells her the news about Vronsky's departure with the volunteers, and takes everyone on a picnic. Discussing the Slavic cause with Sergei, Levin states his opposition to the war and expresses skepticism about the Russian people being unanimously behind it. He tries to argue but realizes he is helpless against the wits of the more intellectual Sergei and Katavasov.

A sudden, violent thunderstorm overtakes the picnickers, who run for the house. Levin learns that Kitty and Mitya are not inside, as he believed, but are still out in the woods. Seeing a giant oak toppling over near where Kitty and the child were sitting, he fears they have been killed but runs to them and finds them safe. Levin realizes the extent of his love for his son, and Kitty is grateful that he finally feels paternal emotions. Feeling another surge of faith, Levin contemplates telling Kitty of his newfound spirituality but decides not to, concluding that faith is private and inexpressible. He feels once again that the meaning of life lies in the goodness that one puts into it.

ANALYSIS

Tolstoy's decision to end the novel with Levin's religious regeneration, rather than with Anna's demise, perplexes many readers who expect the novel to be first and foremost about Anna and her tragedy. The ending shows us yet again that *Anna Karenina* is a novel of ideas, rather than merely a tragic love story. The final chapters recounting Levin's thoughts and feelings as he discovers the meaning of life are more abstract than any other part of the novel, and some paragraphs read like a philosophy treatise. The result is striking: Anna is hardly mentioned in the last part of the novel that bears her name. As Tolstoy clearly intends this omission, we must conclude that he means us to forget or bypass Anna's life—at least in part—in the context of the novel's search for higher meaning. When Levin comes to reject a life lived simply to satisfy one's own desires, he does not mention Anna, but we inevitably think of her. Tolstoy invites us to think that Anna, like Stiva and Dolly's naughty children who destroy things in pursuit of pleasure, has pursued her passion selfishly and destructively. Anna is the negative example of what Levin positively illustrates—the ability to live one's life in commitment to something higher than oneself.

The question of the meaning of life confronts not only Levin, but Sergei and Vronsky as well, and the latter two men come up with quite different answers to the question than Levin does. Vronsky's response is the simpler of the two: he concludes that life has no meaning whatsoever—a notion that Levin fleetingly embraces during his thoughts of suicide. Ironically, this pessimistic idea fuels Vronsky's courageous show of valor in traveling to fight in the Serbian war. Vronsky frankly informs Sergei that the prospect of losing one's life is easy to accept when nothing in life has value. Sergei's conclusion is more complex. Having tried and failed to acquire meaning through intellectual achievement, Sergei masks his private disappointment by throwing himself into a public, patriotic cause. Sergei is not exactly insincere in supporting the Serbians, but his fervor appears shallow, especially when Levin cross-examines him on whether the newspapers have sensationalized the Serbian affair to boost their circulation. Sergei tries to connect with something larger than himself but does so in the wrong way. The humans for whom he cares are abstract, not real. Like Vronsky, Sergei is unable to find good in actual relationships with living humans.

Some feminist critics feel that *Anna Karenina*, though it frequently presents the issue of women's rights with sympathy and fairness, betrays a misogynistic streak at the end. Tolstoy's parallel plot device disappears as the female story line vanishes—Anna is hardly mentioned—leaving the male Levin the star of the show. His reproach to Kitty for taking the baby to the woods against his orders suggests that father knows best, not mother. Likewise, Levin experiences religious enlightenment but decides not to share it with his wife on the grounds that she would not understand it. No woman in the novel has any grand philosophical illumination; they simply have children and busy themselves with domestic concerns. Even Anna's rich experience seems dismissed at the end of the novel. All the compassion with which Tolstoy has represented the complexity of Anna's situation goes up in smoke when Countess Vronsky is given the last word, calling Anna lowly and mean. We know the Countess is wrong, aware of Anna's high-mindedness and nobility, yet nobody in the novel defends Anna or refutes the Countess. In the end, it is as if Tolstoy condemns the female right to seek passion and autonomy—even after leading us to support Anna's claim to that right.

SUMMARY & ANALYSIS

Important Quotations Explained

1. All happy families are alike; each unhappy family is unhappy in its own way.

These famous opening lines of *Anna Karenina* hearken back to the genre of the family novel, a type of work that had been popular in Russia several decades earlier but was already outmoded by the 1870s. Tolstoy revisits this old genre in order to give his own spin on family values, which were a popular target of attack for young Russian liberals at the time. Moreover, this opening sentence of *Anna Karenina* sets a philosophical tone that persists throughout the work. It is not a narrative beginning that tells a story about particular characters and their actions. Rather, it is a generalization, much like a philosophical or scientific argument. It makes a universal statement and is set in the present tense rather than the novelist's preferred past tense. Tolstoy thus announces that he is more than just a novelist, and that his aims are greater than simply weaving a tale for us. He wants us to philosophize about happiness, in the grand tradition set by the philosopher Plato two thousand years earlier.

Yet it is no simple matter to relate this statement about family happiness to the novel as a whole. It is difficult to test the validity of the straightforward assertion that all happy families are alike, as we do not encounter any ideally happy families in *Anna Karenina*. The Oblonskys are torn apart by adultery and financial problems; the Karenins separate in scandal; and even Levin's happy marriage suffers jealous fits and frequent quarrels. Moreover, Tolstoy's statement produces mixed reactions in us: we want to be happy but we do not wish to be exactly like everyone else. The only way to preserve one's uniqueness—in one's "own way"—is by accepting unhappiness. This double bind is the same dilemma that the newly married Levin feels when he struggles between domestic satisfaction on one hand and the need for independence and individualism on the other. It is Tolstoy's version of the Christian idea of original sin: what makes us unique and human is also that which exiles us from happiness.

2.   In that brief glance Vronsky had time to notice the restrained animation that played over her face and fluttered between her shining eyes and the barely noticeable smile that curved her red lips. It was as if a surplus of something so overflowed her being that it expressed itself beyond her will, now in the brightness of her glance, now in her smile.

These lines in Part One, Chapter XVIII, detail the first fateful meeting between Anna and Vronsky at the train station. Tolstoy's description recalls the stereotype of "love at first sight" popular in romance novels of both Tolstoy's day and our own time. In the case of Vronsky and Anna, they share much more than a glance, as both are immediately captivated. Red lips and shining eyes are traditional attributes of the romantic heroine. The device of showing the male as the active looker and the female as the object gazed at is similarly traditional in the romance novel. Words like "fluttered" and "overflowed" might just as easily be found in a trite love scene as in a serious work of literature.

Tolstoy, however, avoids the comic extremes of romance writing by adding a mystical and philosophical dimension to Vronsky and Anna's meeting. The abundance that Anna displays is an excess of "something," a mysterious undefined entity that raises the moment into the realm of spiritualism and religion, beyond language and rational thought. Similarly, the "restrained animation" on Anna's face foreshadows the restraint—in the form of laws, social conventions, duties—that she later fights against as she pursues her illicit love with Vronsky. The description also emphasizes Anna's "animation," her life force, with a word that in both Russian and English is derived from the word for soul. Even in the first moment of Vronsky and Anna's meeting we sense that much more than a physical passion is at stake: their interaction is a study of the soul and the indefinable spiritual qualities that, for Tolstoy, make humans human.

3. "Respect was invented to cover the empty place where love should be. But if you don't love me, it would be better and more honest to say so."

In these lines from Part Seven, Chapter XXIV, Anna reproaches Vronsky for putting his mother's needs before hers. When Vronsky asks to postpone their move to the country a few days so that he can transact some business for Countess Vronsky first, Anna objects, prompting Vronsky to say it is a pity Anna does not respect his mother. Anna's response dismisses the very notion of respect in a rather surprising way. First, Anna makes an irrational connection between Vronsky's mother in the first sentence and herself in the second. Anna refers to the lack of love Vronsky must feel for his mother and then immediately—saying "But" as if continuing the same thought—refers to his lack of love for herself, Anna. We see clearly that, as in many marital quarrels, the apparent topic of conversation (Vronsky's respect for his mother) thinly covers the underlying topic of the spouses' relationship. Second, Anna's contrast between respect and love is startling, even illogical. Most of us value respect and do not consider it the opposite of love or a substitute for love. But we must remember Anna's situation: respect is a public virtue, while love is a private one, and Anna is an outcast from society with no hopes of public pardon. We cannot blame her for hating the social respect that will never be hers again. Moreover, Anna's anger at Vronsky retains traces of her frustration with Karenin. Respectability is Karenin's great concern, often to the detriment of his private life, as when he prefers keeping a rotten marriage that looks respectable to an honest divorce that would have the potential to accommodate love.

QUOTATIONS

4.   "No, you're going in vain," she mentally addressed a
      company in a coach-and-four who were evidently
      going out of town for some merriment. "And the dog
      you're taking with you won't help you. You won't get
      away from yourselves."

These are among Anna's thoughts as she rides to the train station in
Part Seven, Chapter XXX, in one of the most famous interior mono-
logues in the history of literature. On the simplest level, Anna displays a classic case of what the psychoanalyst Sigmund Freud called
projection: she superimposes her own life crisis on others, assuming
that they are as unable to find happiness as she is. In her current
state, Anna is gloomily self-centered, unable to see beyond her own
misery or to acknowledge that other moods or states of mind are
possible. She sums up this self-centered aspect of her unhappiness
perfectly when she mentally informs the others that they cannot get
away from themselves: the self is the center of Anna's existence and
its central problem. She sacrifices friends and family in order to pursue her deepest personal desires and to realize herself, only to discover that her self is her greatest torment—and she cannot get away
from herself except in suicide.

    Anna's words also ironically echo Levin's spiritual meditations.
Her despairing lament that life's activities are all "in vain" is an
expression of the old Christian idea of life's futility—that existence
has no rational aim and therefore must be backed up by faith. It is
this conclusion that Levin makes in realizing that he lives happily
only when he stops analyzing his life rationally. He is able to stop
obsessing about life's futility by simply accepting life and living it in
faith. Anna and Levin mirror each other's experiences, though from
different angles and with very different results.

5. "... [M]y life now, my whole life, regardless of all
    that may happen to me, every minute of it, is not only
    not meaningless, as it was before, but has the
    unquestionable meaning of the good which it is in my
    power to put into it!"

In the closing lines of *Anna Karenina,* Levin's exuberant affirmation of his new faith and philosophy of life reminds us of Tolstoy's aim for his novel, which is philosophical as much as narrative. A typical novel might have ended with Anna's dramatic suicide, but Tolstoy's work concludes with an abstract philosophical statement. Levin's meditation also provides a final instance of how his experiences mirror Anna's. His beginning reflects Anna's end. Levin gains a claim to "my whole life . . . every minute of it" shortly after Anna has utterly lost her whole life. Levin's gain corresponds precisely to Anna's loss, in a symmetry typical of Tolstoy's careful structuring of the novel.

Levin's concluding meditation also mirrors Anna's last thoughts in its focus on the self. Just as Anna, on her fateful ride to the station, fixates on how we cannot escape ourselves, affirming darkly that we are always our own worst enemies, Levin also asserts here the central place of the self in existence. The difference is that Levin finds the self to be not a punisher, as Anna does, but a nurturer that puts value into life, as a farmer—such as Levin himself—puts seeds into the ground. Anna's self is a destroyer, while Levin's is a creator. Both selves are paramount in defining the reality of one's existence. This focus on the self as the center of existence links Tolstoy with the literary modernists that followed him, and helps explain Tolstoy's monumental impact on twentieth-century literature and thought.

QUOTATIONS

KEY FACTS

FULL TITLE
Anna Karenina

AUTHOR
Lev (Leo) Nikolaevich Tolstoy

TYPE OF WORK
Novel

GENRE
Novel of ideas; psychological novel; tragedy

LANGUAGE
Russian

TIME AND PLACE WRITTEN
1873–1877; the estate of Yasnaya Polyana, near Moscow

DATE OF FIRST PUBLICATION
1873–1877 (serial publication)

PUBLISHER
M. N. Katkov

NARRATOR
Tolstoy uses an unnamed, omniscient, detached, third-person narrator

POINT OF VIEW
The nameless narrator of the novel presents both facts and inner thoughts of characters that no single character in the plot could know. Chiefly with regard to Anna and Levin, but occasionally to others as well, the narrator describes characters' states of mind, feelings, and attitudes. For a lengthy section at the end of Part Seven, the narrator enters directly into Anna's mind.

TONE

As in many realist novels of the same time period, the narrator maintains an impersonal but sympathetic tone, focusing on both facts and feelings but without authorial commentaries on the fates of characters. Unlike *War and Peace* and some of Tolstoy's other earlier novels, *Anna Karenina* does not include explicit philosophical generalizations, except in the opening sentence of the novel.

TENSE

Past

SETTING (TIME)

The 1870s

SETTING (PLACE)

Various locations throughout Russia, including Moscow, St. Petersburg, and the Russian provinces, with brief interludes in Germany and Italy

PROTAGONISTS

Anna Karenina; Konstantin Levin

MAJOR CONFLICT

Anna struggles between her passion for Vronsky and her desire for independence on the one hand, and her marital duty, social convention, and maternal love on the other; Levin struggles to define his own identity and reach an understanding of faith in an alienating and confusing world

RISING ACTION

Anna meets Vronsky in the train station, initiating an acquaintance that grows into adulterous passion and family upheaval; their consummation of the affair leads to Anna's abandonment of her husband and son. Meanwhile, Kitty rebuffs Levin's marriage proposal, prompting him to withdraw to his estate in the country and reflect on the meaning of life.

KEY FACTS

CLIMAX

Anna makes a public appearance at the opera, forcing a confrontation between her desire to live life on her own terms and the hostile opinions of St. Petersburg society, which scorns and rejects her; this episode seals her fate as a social outcast and fallen woman. Meanwhile, Levin's search for meaning is rewarded by marriage to Kitty, stable family life, and an understanding of faith.

FALLING ACTION

Anna commits suicide, unable to bear her lack of social freedom and the jealousy and suspicion arising from her unstable relationship with Vronsky. Meanwhile, Levin continues his new life as enlightened husband, father, and landowner.

THEMES

Social change in nineteenth-century Russia; the blessings of family life; the philosophical value of farming

MOTIFS

The interior monologue; adultery; forgiveness

SYMBOLS

Trains; Vronsky's racehorse; Levin and Kitty's marriage

FORESHADOWING

A man dies at the train station when Anna first arrives, foreshadowing her own death at a train station years later; Vronsky's actions cause the fall and death of his horse Frou-Frou, foreshadowing the later death of his beloved Anna.

Study Questions & Essay Topics

Study Questions

1. *There are two main plotlines in* Anna Karenina *— one involving Anna and Vronsky, the other involving Levin and Kitty. These two threads run parallel for most of the novel but occasionally intersect. Where are these intersections? What purpose do they serve in the overall scheme of the novel?*

Tolstoy explained in a famous letter—in response to a reviewer who accused the author of not structuring the plot of *Anna Karenina* carefully enough—that the Anna and Levin story lines are the two "vaults" of the novel but that the intersection or "cornerstone" joining them is not immediately visible. We must search out this intersection. The moments of the plot at which the two stories come together are few: Vronsky's initial courtship of Kitty is one, and Levin's meeting with Anna is another. The latter scene is loaded with importance for us, but the former occurs before we know how the plot will develop, so it is the more easily forgotten instance of crossover. But this former scene is nonetheless of great importance. When we consider what a marriage between Vronsky and Kitty might have been like, we are forced to assess the differences between Anna and Kitty as romantic partners for Vronsky—as well as the differences between Vronsky and Levin as mates for Kitty. While Kitty is instinctively comfortable with and sympathetic to Levin, she feels a strong romantic and sensual pull toward Vronsky. As Tolstoy repeatedly hints that good marriages are founded not on romance but on trusting companionship, we are invited to see Vronsky's rejection of Kitty as a blessing in disguise, saving her from the deceptive lures of romantic passion. Likewise, Vronsky's life with Kitty likely would have been more traditional and stable, and probably happier—though perhaps less rich and varied—than his life with Anna. In a life with the somewhat pedestrian Kitty, Vronsky surely would not have settled in Italy, started painting, or embarked on his grand hospital building project. It is Anna who nourishes such ambitions in him. Such "what if" questions, prompted by Tolstoy's early but momentary joining of Vronsky and Kitty, encourage us to compare, analyze, and reflect in the way that a profound novel of ideas demands.

2. *Though we might expect Anna and Vronsky's flight to Italy to be an important turning point in* Anna Karenina, *in fact very little takes place in the Italian section of the novel. Why does Tolstoy bypass such a potential for drama by making the Italian sojourn so uneventful?*

Tolstoy's decision to send Anna and Vronsky to Italy on their would-be honeymoon is an intentional attempt to set us up for disappointment—a disappointment that is crucial for our understanding of how ill-fated their relationship is. Italy, associated with romance and passion in Tolstoy's time as much as now, figured as a dreamy paradise for lovers in popular love stories of the time. On one hand, Tolstoy purposely plays on that stereotype by sending his loving couple there, showing Anna happy in her Italian palazzo. On the other hand, he plays against the stereotype by presenting Anna and Vronsky's Italian experience as curiously empty and uneventful. Indeed, their stay in Italy is less the grand culmination of their affair than an extended pause that makes us—and perhaps the lovers, too—wonder what will come next. They have little to do in Italy besides stroll, dabble at painting, and buy works of art. There are no fancy dress balls, officers' races, or any of the other venues for social interaction that filled their lives before. The lack is noticeable.

What is missing in Italy, then, is Anna's and Vronsky's integration into society as a couple. Curiously, the very thing they have yearned to escape—Russian society—is what earlier gave structure and meaning to their existences. Italy cannot provide this structure, as Anna and Vronsky do not join Italian society and do not even seem to meet any Italians—not one Italian is fleshed out as a character in this section. The couple lives in a social vacuum, and the emptiness of their experience foreshadows the disappointments of their later life as outsiders to society.

3. *The sudden turn toward the broad nationalism and politics of the "Slavic question" at the end of the novel comes as a stark contrast with the more family-based, personal focus of the earlier parts of the novel. Why might Tolstoy end his novel about happiness and the meaning of life with this thematic twist?*

Though Tolstoy was sympathetic to the plight of Slavic peoples under Turkish rule, he was skeptical of all nationalistic and patriotic bandwagons. He saw such group movements as based on a fantasy of solidarity rather than on actual, loving relationships between humans. He opposed war in general, later inspiring Gandhi with his pacifism, and wished to convey this sentiment in *Anna Karenina*. Though Tolstoy does not explicitly state his views on the Slavic issue in the novel, we nonetheless get hints that he is not a full supporter. Levin, who is often Tolstoy's alter ego in the novel, opposes the Slavic cause. He complains that the cause purports to act on behalf of the Russian people when in fact most common Russians know nothing about it—the cause is largely a fantasy cooked up by newspapers to boost circulation.

Tolstoy also uses the Slavic question to offer a psychological diagnosis of why men become militant. When Vronsky and Koznyshev both get pulled into the cause of war in defense of the southern Slavs, Tolstoy throws a bit of cold water on their enthusiasm by showing how, in both men's lives, political activism may cover up a traumatic personal loss. Koznyshev endures the devastating realization that his recently published book, a six-year labor of love, is worthless and unread; Vronsky, meanwhile, loses Anna, the love of his life. These losses prompt both men to sign up with the Slavic cause, partly as a means of distracting themselves. In this view of political activism and warfare as substitutes for fulfillment in private life, Tolstoy shows us the illusory side of government and statecraft. What Vronsky and Koznyshev both mistakenly aim for in their political activism is what Levin succeeds in finding in his everyday life—a sense of belonging to something larger than oneself. Koznyshev invents a fantasy of the Slavic people in order to assert his ties to the cause, but it is as mentally fabricated as his earlier research was—not real and experienced as Levin's ties with Kitty, Mitya, and his peasants are. The Slavic cause at the end of the novel reminds us that everyone needs connections with others, but some of us invent false connections rather than seek out real ones.

SUGGESTED ESSAY TOPICS

1. The epigraph that opens *Anna Karenina* is a quotation from the Bible, suggesting that religion will be important in the novel. Yet, although characters often toss off biblical epigrams in casual conversation, Tolstoy makes few direct references to religion or the church. Why might the author begin with a biblical quotation but then fail to affirm traditional religion elsewhere in the novel?

2. Tolstoy often gives us access to Vronsky's inner thoughts, but near the end of the novel he does not, leaving us wondering what Vronsky feels as he endures Anna's jealousy and anger. We do not know whether the outwardly cool Vronsky is seething with resentment, generous with sympathy, or patiently gritting his teeth. Why does Tolstoy hide Vronsky's thoughts from us at such a key moment in the novel?

3. Law, religion, and society all harshly condemn Anna's adultery. But her brother, Stiva, is also an adulterer, cheating on Dolly not once but twice. Stiva's case is punished much less severely. Why and how does Tolstoy contrast these cases of adultery that have such different consequences?

4. Tolstoy wrote *Anna Karenina* at a time when Russia was struggling with questions about how to relate to western Europe—whether it should imitate the West or follow a unique path. How do the two major western European episodes in the novel (Kitty at the German spa, Anna and Vronsky in Italy) contribute to Tolstoy's exploration of the relationship between Russia and the West?

5. Critics are divided in their assessments of the novel's overall views of women. Tolstoy shows sympathy for women who suffer in arranged, passionless marriages and who are shunned by society for the same crimes that men commit with impunity. However, many readers have felt that Tolstoy bears a grudge against women and that Anna's suicide is an expression of misogyny. On the whole, do you consider the novel feminist, misogynist, or neutral in its stance?

REVIEW & RESOURCES

QUIZ

1. What good deed does Anna do when she visits the Oblonsky household in Part One?

   A. She nurses their daughter back to health
   B. She offers them financial assistance
   C. She brings husband and wife back together
   D. She helps them sell a forest on their estate

2. Who is Frou-Frou?

   A. A dog
   B. A cow
   C. A horse
   D. A cat

3. Where do Anna and Vronsky first meet?

   A. On the street
   B. At the opera
   C. At a horse race
   D. At a train station

4. How are Stiva and Anna related?

   A. They are brother and sister
   B. They are husband and wife
   C. They are cousins
   D. They are father and daughter

5. What is the subject of the book Levin plans to write?

   A. Medicine
   B. Agriculture
   C. History
   D. Philosophy

6. In which country do Vronsky and Anna spend most of their time in Europe?

    A. France
    B. Italy
    C. Austria
    D. Spain

7. What happens at the train station just after Anna's first meeting with Vronsky?

    A. A fire
    B. A death
    C. A riot
    D. A train wreck

8. What is Dolly's maiden name?

    A. Shcherbatskaya
    B. Oblonskaya
    C. Karenina
    D. Tverskaya

9. Where does Anna make her disastrous attempt to rejoin St. Petersburg society after her scandal?

    A. At a garden party
    B. At a governor's ball
    C. At the opera
    D. In a park

10. Who is Seryozha's father?

    A. Karenin
    B. Stiva
    C. Levin
    D. Vronsky

11. What is the result of Vronsky's error at the horse race?

    A. The maiming of Vronsky's groom
    B. The death of Vronsky's horse
    C. Stiva's loss of a large bet
    D. Vronsky's exile from Russia

12. What is Vronsky's career before his resignation?

    A. Medicine
    B. Law
    C. Business
    D. The military

13. What does Levin fear during the severe thunderstorm on his estate in the last chapter of the novel?

    A. That his wife and son have been hurt
    B. That his fields have been flooded
    C. That his house has been hit by lightning
    D. That his dog has been stranded

14. What does Levin's half-brother, Koznyshev, do?

    A. He is a farmer
    B. He is a writer and philosopher
    C. He is a lawyer
    D. He is a government official

15. What was Marya Nikolaevna's profession when Nikolai Levin met her?

    A. Schoolteacher
    B. Nurse
    C. Maid
    D. Prostitute

16. What is the name of Levin and Kitty's child?

    A. Mitya
    B. Grisha
    C. Annie
    D. Tanya

17. Who, besides Levin, courts Kitty?

    A. Vronsky
    B. Stiva
    C. Karenin
    D. Veslovsky

REVIEW & RESOURCES

18. What does Vronsky have made in Italy?

    A.   A wardrobe for Anna
    B.   A luxury carriage
    C.   A portrait of Anna
    D.   A set of china

19. What does Veslovsky do to anger Levin?

    A.   He is rude to Levin's servants
    B.   He expresses objectionable political views
    C.   He expects Levin to pay his gambling debts
    D.   He flirts with Kitty

20. Which pursuit does Anna take up during her life with Vronsky?

    A.   Writing a children's book
    B.   Breeding roses
    C.   Overseeing peasant education
    D.   Playing the piano

21. What cause sweeps Russia in the final section of the novel?

    A.   The Franco-Prussian war
    B.   The Serbian war
    C.   The Russian presidential elections
    D.   The conquest of central Asia

22. Where does Anna die?

    A.   At home
    B.   In the Oblonsky house
    C.   On the street
    D.   At a train station

23. In the last chapter of the novel, what does Levin finally feel he understands?

    A.   Why Anna killed herself
    B.   Why Kitty originally rejected him
    C.   Why Russian agriculture fails
    D.   What faith is

24. What does the psychic Landau instruct Karenin to do?

    A. Take Anna back as his wife
    B. Reject Anna's plea for a divorce
    C. Fight for a post on the government train commission
    D. Give up custody of Seryozha

25. What characteristic of Varenka's does Kitty appreciate while at the German spa?

    A. Her good deeds
    B. Her fashion sense
    C. Her ability to attract male attention
    D. Her intellectual curiosity

SUGGESTIONS FOR FURTHER READING

CRANKSHAW, EDWARD. *Tolstoy: The Making of a Novelist.* New York: Viking, 1974.

GUNN, ELIZABETH. *A Daring Coiffeur: Reflections on* WAR AND PEACE *and* ANNA KARENINA. London: Chatto and Windus, 1971.

MANDELKER, AMY. *Framing* ANNA KARENINA: *Tolstoy, the Woman Question, and the Victorian Novel.* Columbus: University of Ohio Press, 1993.

MOONEY, HARRY J. *Tolstoy's Epic Vision: A Study of* WAR AND PEACE *and* ANNA KARENINA. Tulsa: University of Oklahoma Press, 1968.

SANKOVITCH, NATASHA. *Creating and Recovering Experience: Repetition in Tolstoy.* Palo Alto, California: Stanford University Press, 1998.

SHIRER, WILLIAM L. *Love and Hatred: The Troubled Marriage of Leo and Sonya Tolstoy.* New York: Simon and Schuster, 1994.

TROYAT, HENRI. *Tolstoy.* Garden City, New York: Doubleday, 1967.

TURNER, C.J.G. *A Karenina Companion.* Waterloo, Ontario: Wilfrid Laurier University Press, 1993.